Praise for *Darker E...*

"Diverse, edgy, and infused with fantasy and horror, this chilling anthology of incendiary short stories is certainly not your typical Halloween romance anthology, but it will appeal to fans of the dark, erotic, and forbidden who don't expect traditional love stories or 'happily ever afters.'"

—*Library Journal*

"When your midnight cravings come calling, *Darker Edge of Desire* is the book you want on your nightstand. Wedged between these covers are fourteen tales of seduction and submission, from lust most carnal to virginal awakenings— and even (despite the title) moments of achingly tender sweetness. *Darker Edge of Desire* is a chocolate box assortment of stories that depict passion in all its varieties, most—but not all—of them with a supernatural twist, no two of them the same. Bon appétit."

—Alma Katsu, author of The Taker Trilogy

DARKER EDGE OF DESIRE

GOTHIC TALES OF ROMANCE

Edited by Mitzi Szereto

Foreword by Kate Douglas
Afterword by Rachel Caine

**TEMPTED
ROMANCE**

Published in the United States by Tempted Romance, an imprint of
Cleis Press, Inc., 2246 Sixth Street, Berkeley, California 94710.

Printed in the United States.
Cover design: Scott Idleman/Blink
Cover photograph: D. Sharon Pruitt/Getty Images
Text design: Frank Wiedemann

First Edition.
10 9 8 7 6 5 4 3 2 1

Trade paper ISBN: 978-1-940550-00-8
E-book ISBN: 978-1-940550-05-3

Contents

If a thing loves, it is infinite.
—William Blake

Foreword

Kate Douglas

I am not by nature a fan of the Gothic tale or the truly dark story, not with my unwavering Pollyanna personality and unwillingness to connect with the darkness, and yet there are those times when I find the darkness appealing—compelling, actually. Those times when I see it as another side of the same coin—just as powerful, just as necessary, just as strongly desired. It's as if those tales of death and demons, of devils and depravity touch a part of the soul that occasionally needs to be reminded evil does exist. That without evil, there would be nothing truly good because the one must flourish to give its opposite a reason to exist.

A counterweight. The concept of yin and yang. The idea that opposites are interconnected, that you can't have one without the other. It's all about balance, and yet the one thing that can come closest to tipping that delicate scale is sexual desire: visceral, soul-searing arousal so all-consuming in its power that it can drag a soul from the heights of ecstasy into the darkness of absolute despair, or lift that same soul from hopeless desperation into unfathomable joy. The fascination lies in the journey, the choices that are made, the actions taken.

Standing on the precipice, balanced precariously between good and evil, every protagonist in any situation has a choice to make—leaping one way or the other, toward the darkness or into the light. But when the lure of darkness is swathed in sexual desire and soul-searing need, the balance is compromised, especially when leaping into the abyss can bring pleasure well beyond any mortal concept of heaven. Love and desire can cruelly twist the best of intentions, or they can build armor impervious to whatever twisted weapons evil might bring to bear against them.

Twisted? Yes, desire can be so intricately, beautifully twisted, so perfect in its dark and dangerous attraction that there exists no other choice but to follow that compelling lure, follow without regard to safety or personal danger. Arousal, the body's clamor for completion, the mind's desire for answers, the soul's need for fulfillment—all acting in that unifying drive for consummation of desire.

So often our everyday lives have become bland: a process of survival, going off to work, taking care of family, putting meals on the table, going to bed and then getting up and doing it all over again. The highs and lows, the darkness and the light have faded into featureless shades of gray and beige. But knowing the darkness is out there, believing in the sensual lure of danger and desire, that overwhelming arousal that heightens the senses and increases the heart rate—just knowing the darkness exists, gives reason for hope.

Because if the darkness is there, tugging at the edges of the bland landscapes of our lives, then the promise of completion remains. The highs and lows, desires and fears that bring seasoning to a tasteless existence, are still swirling and seething—out there, yet still within reach. And if that seasoning exists, so does the hope for something more.

Desire isn't always fulfilled. It isn't always perfect, and sometimes *Darker Edge of Desire* leads down paths better *not* traveled. And yet the lure is powerful, the path well marked, the warnings clear. Following that twisted, dark and dangerous way is rife with promise and tainted with despair, but always there is hope. Hope for something more, for something sublime.

All you need do is put fear aside and step into the dark.

Kate Douglas
Author of the Wolf Tales series

Introduction

Desire. We've all felt it, experienced it, been tormented by it. It's the most normal and natural of human emotions. Desire can be many things to each of us, appearing in various forms and at various points throughout our lives. Often it might just sit there, simmering beneath the surface until such time as it can be safely brought to fulfillment.

But there are times when that desire becomes darker and more forbidden. And then it can be so much *more*...

Gothic literature has always possessed a dark attraction ripe with the promise of the forbidden and the sensual, using desire as its key motivating force. This theme has been successfully explored in my anthology *Red Velvet and Absinthe*, though with a slightly gentler touch. In *Darker Edge of Desire*, I have taken the sexualized Gothic and ratcheted it up a few notches into the danger zone, opening the door to a side of lust and love that only the most courageous dare to venture through. Here you will find stories with some very sharp edges as well as those that possess the haunting subtlety of the classics.

In these fourteen tales love and lust know no boundaries, and all forms of creature—from the corporeal to the supernatural—can be found. *Darker Edge of Desire* will introduce you to demons, shape shifters, werewolves, immortal beings, automata, ghostly spirits, vampires and even creatures never conceived of in your most disturbing dreams. You will also be introduced to everyday women and men who have found themselves walking down a pathway into darkness. And indeed, there are even some who prefer to remain there!

Passion is the driving force behind each story, leading to events that don't always end well, though there are still some happy endings to be found. We see this passion revealing itself in such places as a candlelit cellar featuring strange erotic rituals; a woodland populated with howling coyotes; a mysterious underworld filled with steam and fire; the isolated villages and cemeteries of Transylvania; a castle made from rose-colored glass; the teeming streets of nineteenth-century Baltimore; old New England with its spells and potions; and even the segregated American South. And let's not forget those classic Gothic favorites, the drafty old manor house and Victorian asylum.

Darker Edge of Desire contains an international and diverse cast of writers, resulting in a unique and exciting collection of sexy Gothic tales guaranteed to titillate and thrill as they take you into dark places you'll not easily forget.

So turn up the light in your oil lantern. It's time to get reading!

Mitzi Szereto
(Writing from an undisclosed location in the Carpathian Mountains)

The Wicked Wife

T. C. Mill

S he looked forward to her wedding night with Andrew Cobalt as she never had with her first husband.

Aria sat at her dressing table, brushing her hair. Uncut since before her first marriage, it fell to the floor in a rich, satiny river the color of oak wood. Andrew came in silently, without the train of revelers customarily accompanying a bridegroom, but she saw him in the mirror.

She thought of him as young, though he was only so by comparison. Gray frosted his thick black hair. His whippet-thin body was a scholar's, but kept fit by frequent exercise. His open collar revealed a tanned chest, rippled with patterns of muscle.

She turned to greet him. "Good night, Andrew."

"Good night, Berengaria."

"Please, call me Aria. Berengaria is a long-dead queen."

A tight smile crossed his face as he went to the bed. He lay down, opening his collar farther—idly, for his own comfort. He waited, neither summoning nor inviting her. He knew she would come.

Aria put down her brush and said, "This is a lovely house."

"Purchased from a recluse, or perhaps his executors. It has been well kept, and the solitude may be welcome." Wiry fingers traced the embroidery on her pillows. "Does it please you, Aria?" A slight hesitation before he said the name, but his fingers never stopped stroking, petting insensate silk.

She rose and came to him. "It does," she said.

Andrew undressed, pulling the shirt over his head before she could reach for it. This bared more of the compactly powerful build she'd glimpsed—along with, in a jagged line across his lower ribs, a silver scar.

Aria traced it, raising shivers, until he captured her hand. "That was a long time ago," he said.

She looked into his eyes—dark, and with a gleam like new ice over deep water. "And now...?"

He bent forward to kiss her and reached for the hem of her nightgown.

His fingers skimmed her flesh with the same ungentle, almost impersonal touch with which he'd graced the coverlet. Not that he was brutal or cruel; the pressure became lighter, slower as he skimmed her private folds, slipped between them to massage the threshold of her channel. Aria spread her legs, smiling simply, honestly, at the pleasant sensation. She'd never felt anything like it before except the weak enjoyment she'd given herself, when her previous husband snored loudly enough that she knew it wouldn't disturb him. Andrew moved with more surety and skill, and complete concentration.

The smile melted away as his thumb rubbed her rosebud swell in small, sweet circles that brought the heat pooling between her thighs. Desire was a heavy ache; dew beaded over his stroking fingers. Andrew's breathing changed as he felt it, becoming shorter and harsher.

Aria opened herself to him, and once his finger pressed inside, *right* where she wanted him, she reached down and grasped his wrist, guiding. Between the two of them they soon had her riding his hand. She had never, ever done anything of the kind before, but it was natural, obedience to an irresistible impulse. No doubt Cobalt was surprised to discover he had such a wanton wife—though not, Aria thought as she caught a glimpse of his expression through the haze of her own pleasure, disappointed. His fingers flexed inside her, stealing her breath, but it was too late to try to tame the creature they'd let loose—if he even wanted to try.

Some men would be uneasy at awakening such passion in a woman, something they couldn't control. Aria's first husband would have been, if he'd ever managed. But Andrew Cobalt caught fire from it. After withdrawing only long enough to strip off his trousers, he kissed her—briefly, but not dispassionately, with soft lips—and pressed her inner thighs, spread her folds. His thumb met her nub again as he sheathed himself, toyed with her as she exclaimed, riding out the new sensation. Just as they built it, the rhythm fractured, ceased as he lost himself in her. Bewildered herself, Aria slid her fingers down between their bodies to finish the job as her other hand grasped his hip, urging him on until her nails dug in.

He had not exactly proven a biddable husband so far, except in this. And here was one task—now that she had such a handsome, vibrant partner—where she could not be a demure bride. Yet it seemed they were both satisfied. She mused as she lay with Cobalt's arm wrapped around her waist like an iron band, his head pillowed on her breast and one hand stroking her long hair, which lay over their naked bodies like a blanket. Yes, this could be quite a satisfactory marriage. Well worth replacing her old one.

Aria hadn't planned to marry again after her first husband's death. It had been such a strain to her, frankly, that once it was over she desired nothing more than peaceful retirement on the simple estate he left her, having no other heirs. Seclusion came naturally—never having a chance for sociability as Bannerman Lowell's wife, she found her few acquaintances melted away as the whisperings started.

Poison, they said. Well, of a sort. The old man's aversion to walnuts proved rooted in sound sense, as the chopped handful in his tart of one evening cut off his breath with alarming swiftness. Aria had not put them there, and was disgusted at the insinuations that she had, frustrated that civility dictated she must never mention those rumors, enraged that no one would believe her disavowal, anyway. What sort of woman would murder her husband just because he bored her?

Yet it was true she had kept quiet about the cook's mistake. The poor man had suffered enough—and even worse had been the lot of his daughter, the laundry maid that Bannerman had taken to visiting of nights. It had been a relief for Aria, spared that tedious duty. But unkind to the girl—she could admit that now, after it was all past.

Andrew Cobalt had come up to the secluded township with a friend for the autumn hunt, and chance brought them near Aria's cottage. She offered the men refreshment, and they'd spoken of the weather, of luck with the game.

Cobalt listened more than spoke, but sat up straighter when he heard her name: Berengaria Lowell. He'd heard the rumors, perhaps. His friend cared nothing of them, because her ale was good (and he could stomach walnuts, he'd once told her with an irreverent laugh, without trouble). But Cobalt seemed the sort to care—and not distracted by the quality of the ale—and so once he left, Aria had not expected to see him again.

It disappointed her.

Yet, not many days later, a servant came to her door with a message from Andrew Cobalt, asking permission to visit. Aria granted it. She drew more drink from the cellar. She combed out her hair and braided it with two spans of scarlet ribbon.

Surely Cobalt noticed, but he was not rude enough to stare. They spoke of inconsequential things—how his hunt had gone, prospects for the harvest. She served him cool cider with her own hands and he did not hesitate to drink it. When he was gone, she spent the evening reliving the sound of his voice as he said unimportant words.

And then he came again.

They spoke more, laughing sometimes. They drank and ate together. And it was after several weeks of this that he asked to marry her.

He asked. Aria clung to this proof that he wanted her, the man she wanted more than she'd ever imagined wanting a man before, and he wanted her despite the ugly, dogging rumors.

He'd proven passionate in her bed and kindly enough elsewhere. His courtesy, she felt certain, was sincere; at times that was all that differentiated this marriage from her first. That and the fact that he seemed disinclined to bother servant girls.

Days passed in which they said not five words to each other, despite nights in which they knew each other as if they were the last two creatures on the earth. When she came upon him in a room he looked up as if at an interruption, and though often he smiled afterward, it was clear the interruption was unwelcome. Even after they made love, he would not lie long in her arms before moving away with a sigh; in the morning a gray and melancholy mood would hang around him. Once she tried to tease him out of it, asking his help to comb her long hair. He gave it, moving the brush in long, firm strokes, letting the rich strands fall between his fingers. But then he left, and the look on his face was such that she never dared ask him again.

That was new; her presence never had made her last husband gray and melancholy.

It was almost a relief when Andrew Cobalt took a hunting trip in the month after their wedding. For the next six or seven days, Aria would be alone in truth.

She decided to spend the time exploring the old manor house. Andrew offered her a tour on their first day as man and wife, but it only covered the main living quarters. There was so much left unseen, perhaps even places *he* did not yet know.

Well then, Aria thought, *I'll be the one leading the next tour. If he trusts me enough to follow me into shadowy spaces.*

The house seemed made of shadowy spaces. Windows, even in the library, were few and thin, while ancient tapestries and heirloom portraits made the walls thirsty for any drop of light. She lit a candelabra from the silver pantry and carried it with her down the west corridor. Many rooms opening onto it were empty, though some, startlingly, teemed with sheeted furniture like ghosts of old occupants.

At first she took the long, white-skirted slab as another such, before noticing the icon above the altar. Breathing shallowly, quietly, Aria stepped into the chapel. She hadn't been near one since her wedding day. God might know she was innocent, but she didn't feel He cared for her all the same.

The cloth was neatly ironed and laundered, the icon clean of dust. She knelt before the altar for a moment, unable to say what brought her to it, and then rose. As she did, she spotted the door.

Low to the ground and small, with streaks of dust clinging to the age-polished oak boards, at first it appeared to be a servant's door—yet what need was there for a chapel to be unobtrusively cleaned and serviced? It was in use mere hours a week.

Something else, then, meant to be unobtrusive.

She approached the strange door, keeping her steps light, as if someone might be listening. She reached out and at her touch it moved inward on its hinges, but not all the way. Holding her breath, Aria grasped the handle and pushed it.

The door swung open onto gray twilight.

High, dusty windows were spaced evenly in the thick stone walls, by which dim illumination she could make out the contents of the room—what little there was. Boxes lined a narrow aisle down the center of the chamber. The wood was sanded smooth but plain, the whole at odds with the elegance of the rest of the house. Perhaps left behind by the place's last owner?

Curious, Aria went to one and, with some straining, lifted its lid.

At first she could make out nothing from the darkness inside, but a smell arose: like dust, but *stickier* in her nose and throat. Coughing to clear it away, she looked down—into a face that was no longer a face.

Gray and withered, flesh like old leather pulled tight across a framework of bones, lying crumbled in the box as if dropped there. The rags, remnants of a gown in the style of fifteen years ago, hung off one skeletal shoulder and with the skirt flipped high, revealing the bones of calves and long feet. A slipper had fallen away, revealing long yellow nails.

Aria fell back, and a sound escaped her throat that was in its way as frightful as the discovery. She viewed the scene as if outside herself—*poor woman, what a shock.* And, from this outside vantage, she was seized with awful curiosity.

She rose and went to another box. Opened it. This one was fresher than the first—more horrible. And another. She stumbled between the two rows, revealing their burdens as if hoping the next would prove her wrong. Finding the dead near a chapel was not unusual after all. But these, in their disarray, were too clearly unburied, unhallowed dead.

The last she opened was still recognizable: a young woman in a blue gown, with fair hair falling out of its braids. A bright length crossed her breast—a knife, laid carefully between her hands. Aria didn't dare look to see if its mark was on her flesh.

Stumbling back, she nearly tripped over the plank resting beside the final box in the line. The lid of the coffin, waiting to seal it—whenever the empty thing was filled.

Aria went to her knees, then, and remained there a long time.

Surely this was the work, the terrible secret, of the last master of this house... Perhaps there was even some innocent, obvious explanation, which she had misread in her fright. She would rise from the floor and laugh at herself in a few minutes.

Footsteps intruded on her silence, and brought a rush of instinctive terror. She leapt up, ready to flee. But a figure's bulk blocked the door. To fight, then—a cooler, wiser aspect of Berengaria reached for the blade on the dead woman's chest. She held it before her, mirrored steel casting trembling spots of light across the walls.

One struck the face of Andrew Cobalt.

He blinked against it as he stepped into the room. Aria told herself to put down the knife; this was her husband, danger was past. Cooler, wiser instinct kept the blade between them.

My dear, she expected his parted lips to say. *Oh, my dear, what an awful thing you've found!* Speaking gently, soothingly.

He spoke gently, but the words he said were, "You poor fool."

"Fool?" she asked, voice soaring high into the eaves of the hall. "How?"

Let him tell her she misunderstood.

"You shouldn't have come here. It might have waited a while longer."

"This—surely this belonged to the last owner of this house, the man you bought it from."

Cobalt laughed. "I bought it from myself."

Aria stared at him, and dazedly shook her head.

He came closer. Changed from traveling clothes, he was dressed in a linen shirt, half unlaced, and tight trousers. The simple outfit revealed the muscles of his legs and forearms, below his rolled-up cuffs. His dark hair seemed to drink in the gray light; its gray strands became gilded. He was a stranger, and terrible, and beautiful, too.

"I bought it from a recluse. And he from a merchant who traveled long abroad. Before that, the lucky heir of an unknown uncle. Somewhere among the list, a lord with nothing left of his inheritance but these useless halls." His expression turned thoughtful. "Perhaps not useless...and somewhere, a madman."

"Who were these women?" Aria asked.

"Wives," Cobalt said. "Bad ones."

Hot blood rushed in Aria's cheeks. In contrast, the knife's hilt felt cold and slick. She kept from dropping it with an effort. "Your wives?"

"Not at first."

Oh, thank God. It was all nothing, then.

"It's true they all came to marry me, for the reasons women come to marry men: protection, a need for money or goods—for some, this house—and because of loneliness. When any was lonely, it was her own fault. I was always her second husband."

"Widows." The word squeaked past her tight throat.

"Self-made, each one." He stopped before her, an empty coffin between them. *The* empty coffin. "Murderers, who would have gone unpunished if not for me."

Her coffin.

"I'm not a murderer!" Mixed with Aria's terror burned a blaze of indignation. "It was an accident!"

He began to walk around to her. She dodged, keeping the coffin between them.

"Anyway," she continued, "that vile man deserved to die."

"So you also believe some deaths must happen?" Cobalt smiled. "At least we agree on so much."

He drew too close; she feinted with the knife.

"Sarah's," he said, looking at it with not a little affection mixed with wariness. "Ah, she put up a glorious fight. I still bear the mark of it."

Aria remembered the scar she had traced so sensuously in his bed. A wave—of something that ought to be revulsion, but wasn't—overtook her, and she lowered the blade.

"Some fight," he said, with undeniable fondness now. "Yet

others...offer money, the inheritance from slaughtered men. As if that could dissuade me, either."

"No," she said, realizing. "You've devoted your life to this."

He nodded, pleased they again understood each other. In his intention he was pure, and the austerity that ruled him drew at something within Aria. Standing before her in the tomb he had made, Andrew Cobalt seemed made of equal parts simplicity, strength and inhuman beauty. Like an avenging angel, or a monstrous ancient god.

Aria had never thought herself the sort to bring down angels, and never expected to confront a god. But she remembered her husband's cool decorum, which she had made to melt from him for a night. When he had awakened something more than mortal in her, too.

She stood before what might be her death, and felt life throughout every inch of her body. Passion ached, pulsing with each beat of her heart, through blushing face, along her trembling arms, and at the gate of her womb. She almost staggered with it.

"Others have tried to run," he said. In this he misunderstood her.

Aria didn't flee. Instead she let him come near—which he did, so slowly she must have taken a hundred breaths while waiting—and she let the knife fall. Its clatter against the stones echoed, tones filling the air like music. She let Andrew's hand clasp her by the throat. The instant he did, she stepped closer, into his arms. His heat surrounded her, and her hungry body opened to it, as if her flesh were made of unfolding leaves before his sun. And she kissed him.

He tried to draw away, but she wouldn't let him. He'd left her hands free; she closed one tight on his shoulder, keeping them together, and reached the other down between his legs. He was not like her, charged by facing death; neither was he some crude beast to be excited at the thought of dealing it. But his lips opened to her kiss, at first tolerating it, but quickly revealing more interest. He growled against her mouth, but she felt the surge of arousal through him as she stroked the hard line of his cock through the tight canvas trousers.

His hold slackened enough that she could speak through it, her voice breathless, husky with fear and desire. "We can have this, husband, one last time. At least bid me a good farewell."

Andrew forced her to her knees, and doing so by necessity brought himself down. He had a wiry strength, but not irresistible, not to a woman fighting for her life and whose form of resistance he could not anticipate. And perhaps he did not want to resist, either. She got atop him, straddling his thighs, and unlaced his trousers. Her fingers slipped inside to fondle him, found him hot and hard as an iron blade. Aria flexed her legs to kick her skirts back out of the way and took him into her. He drove home with one sharp thrust—willing, then. Wetness welled from her flesh surrounding him; hope and terror both proved strong aphrodisiacs.

But his grip was closing tight on her throat again. Not tight enough to cut off her life, at least not yet, but the promise was there—once they finished, and completion already rushed toward them. His thrusts came fast, slicked by her arousal. His length spread her open, and caressed every inch exposed to him with overwhelmingly sweet friction. It was bliss, sheer bliss, and she could almost have let it be as she said. A fond farewell, a final rapture before the end.

But Aria wasn't ready for it to end yet. She rose and fell against him, throwing off the rhythm of his thrusts, reshaping the sensations laying siege to her. Distracting him, so that his hold slackened. She gasped in air, as much and as deeply as possible.

Andrew ripped the high collar from around her neck, tore open the front of her gown. He palmed her breast, caressing until the nipple was pinched hard against his warm skin. Pleasure drove the breath from her, and even the grip of his single hand was dangerously firm. Yet pleasure came from that, too, from the sting of her empty lungs. There seemed to be a great distance between the parts of her body—head and throat, teased breast and full, wet quim—but joy, physical joy, danced between and among all of them. Perhaps he felt it, too.

He let her know what he did feel with another hard thrust, and then, perhaps to coax more of the easing dew from her, Andrew bent his head and suckled at her breast. Aria arched back, rising to his attentions. And farther, until he had to shift his hips in longer, higher strokes to remain deep within her. She felt herself flying...then falling, as he came back to himself, tried to take control. She closed her hands behind his back and pulled him down with her, until she lay with only her pooled skirts cushioning her hips from the flagstones and with Cobalt rising over her. He had a better angle now to grip tight on her throat. But she had the advantage of surprise and his distraction. Cobalt moved from instinct, in the age-old pattern—with perhaps a bit of calculation, keeping them both from the edge, keeping his hands on her light enough to keep from making love to a corpse. He plainly found the living woman much preferable—and in his surrender to what she offered, Aria pursued her advantage.

In moments, she had her own noose around his throat— a length of her long hair, looped and coiled tight. Not tight enough to kill; perhaps it was only a collar. Yet a collar was a mark of control, and control Andrew Cobalt she did, riding him from beneath, spurring him to madness. Throwing herself into madness, too. She felt him tremble deep within her, and her intimate muscles shivered around him. She felt his climax come as though it tore the world asunder.

He surged within her. She pulled tight the band of her hair, trying to slow him before he pushed her to annihilation. What saved her in the end, though, was the pain as in his orgasm Andrew's teeth marked the creamy skin of her breast and grazed the areola of her nipple. It was pain less akin to ecstasy than the sweetness of restricted breath had proved, and it was unexpected; the two factors pulled her back from the edge. And then his storm had passed; he lay weakened and helpless in her arms, the last of his release pulsing into her.

She stroked one hand down the length of his slick, well-exercised body; the other kept a firm grip on the end of the collar. Suddenly, she saw it within reach—the knife. The blade that had almost killed him once before.

Andrew's eyes flickered open; he looked in the same direction, and she knew he saw it, too.

She could have taken the knife. Could have ended it there, could have made what they'd just done a farewell in truth, could have saved herself.

But desire still burned in the place where he rested. Urgently, she chased it, moving her hips and savoring the slide of him within—softening, but still large, still filling her in the way she needed. Her breasts dragged across his firm chest. His grip on her throat was joy as pure as any of the rest; she had never felt her life so keenly. A cry escaped her, despite his best attempt to throttle it—if that was, in fact, his best attempt.

Rapture took hold, far stronger and more irresistible than his tightening hands. Swept away for a clean endless moment she knew nothing, had no concern, and the lingering shadow of fear only gilded the brightness surrounding her.

She lay, then, as helpless as Andrew had been, with his fingers banding her throat and the knife as near. Yet she awakened—she came back, feeling washed from the inside out and filled with sweet lassitude like that following a most pleasant dream.

Slowly, Andrew rose and separated from her. Aria looked up at him, waiting.

"Well?" she said as moments passed, sensuality's spell began to weaken on her, and he still did nothing.

"You could have done it," he said. With a booted foot— she had never even tried to unbutton his boots—he kicked the knife. Not away, but nearer to her.

Aria did not reach for it. "I didn't want to."

"No? Not even to save your life?" Breathlessly, with strands of her long hair still falling across his shoulders, he asked, "What *did* you want, then?"

She could only be honest. "You."

"So I saw." Andrew laughed with, she thought, genuine amusement. And he offered her a hand up.

She rose, and though there was no help for her torn, gaping bodice she began shaking her skirts into a more proper array. One slippered foot trod on the hilt of the knife, rested there. "You see, then. I'm not a murderer."

Perhaps she had just tried to become one—but strategy had failed her in the end. As it had failed him.

This time.

Aria frowned at her husband. "Yet you are."

"Ah." Softly, with the realization he was at her mercy: "Aren't we all something less than innocent?"

"So you admit we are all somewhat deserving of clemency?"

She almost couldn't hear his response. "Perhaps none of us deserve it."

He seemed to find the thought terrifying and appealing in equal measure.

Well, she could sympathize.

A red band marked his neck, though already fading: the impression of her collar. Aria smiled at the sight. "Some of us less than others."

"They were truly wicked women, you know."

Were they? She looked around her. Impossible to judge, now—there could be no trials and no second chances for the dead. But Cobalt had taken her on mere rumors of poison. How many others had been condemned by nothing but rumor?

She looked at his bare chest, the scar cutting across it. It had been wielded with no little skill. Not unpracticed, she would say.

Perhaps there had been some justice dealt, then.

And if any were innocent? Could there be justice for them?

Andrew Cobalt looked at her, waiting. Aria reached out, pressed him to his knees. It made him less likely to attempt any dangerous motion...and put his mouth at an interesting level.

Aria was not a murderer, although she had knowingly let a man die when he deserved it.

She could not kill this husband of hers, though, not for anything.

Yet...

"I'm something of a wicked woman, myself," she said. Her hand toyed with the ends of his hair.

Her fingers tightened in the fine strands as he bowed his

head, accepting her judgment. Proving a more biddable husband than she'd at first expected. How refreshing.

Aria drew him nearer to her. This had the makings of a quite satisfactory marriage.

"RED HOUSE"

Zander Vyne

T ony Depapas lusted after his brother's wife. She longed for Tony too, but that made no difference. Both agreed, though neither knew it, never to speak of this attraction. Instead, they offered the required words and left the confessional booth with a penance designed to soothe their troubled minds, though it would do nothing to ease the heat in their loins.

Father Mihalis sighed, eyes closed. The air smelled of dust and sweat. His hands clasped his rosary, drawing smooth black beads over flesh that ached with arthritis, fingers stopping at the cross and working their way back up. His mind had already turned away from the sinners to other, more important, things.

"Frozen lasagna or Benny's Pizza?" he muttered to himself. He started to stand, stiff knees popping in protest.

"In the name of the Father, and of the Son, and of the Holy Spirit. My last confession was...never." The voice was English, cultured, deep and measured in tone.

Another, come late to the party. Typical, Father Mihalis

thought; quick to sin, slow to repent. "I heard the last confession. Contact the office to make an appointment if you are in dire need. Otherwise, I will hear confession again after our next mass," he said, sitting back down.

He never liked facing the sinners on their way out of the confessional. Awkward, it was. Best to let them leave cloaked in the silence of their shame and the glory of their contrition.

This one did not leave, nor did he reply.

Father Mihalis waited him out. He'd had many years to cultivate patience.

He was rewarded when, finally, the Englishman spoke again. "You are inviting me to see you whenever I wish?"

Within reason, Father Mihalis thought. It was with the calm of many years' service to others he replied, "Yes, of course. Anytime." Only later did he think of the odd way the question had been asked after the long, uncomfortable silence.

He waited for the man to speak again, to offer thanks, or perhaps argue for time now, but no words came. He peered through the shadows into the other side of the confessional. After a few minutes, he had to accept that no one was there. Somehow, the man had disappeared without making a sound.

Father Mihalis, or John, as he preferred to be called when he was not in the church, scraped the last of his supper into the trash bin. Lean Cuisine's newest offering had not sat well with his stomach.

His feet made scuffing sounds on the linoleum as he shuffled from the small galley kitchen back into what served as his living room. The church provided meager lodgings, but free was better rent than many paid, and he did not require much room. He had managed to save most of his salary over the years and looked forward to retiring to a warmer clime, perhaps near an ocean where he could afford a large house and a maid to clean it.

The television cast shadows along the walls and ceiling. No other light shined, not even a candle. John liked it dark at night, after being under the bright fluorescents of the church office all day. Even the stained-glass windows tourists gasped over grew tiresome after long enough, the sun making the red glass stab his eyes like knives, causing terrible headaches.

At first, he thought the dark shape in his reclining chair was a shadow. It *had* to be a shadow. Then, it spoke. "Thank you for inviting me into your home."

"Who are you? How dare you? What do you want? Get out!" John shouted, blurting every thought in his head in his panic.

The man did not move. "Please, sit," he said, pointing toward the small chintz-covered chair John reserved for his rare guests.

It was the Englishman, the one who had disappeared from the confessional. The one John had thought of several times since the incident. The one he'd dreamed of, much to his dismay.

"You must leave at once or I shall call the police," John said. It never served to let anyone see your fears, or know your weaknesses. But he had grown old, and it was harder than it once was to hide behind the mask of priesthood, especially here in his ratty old robe and dirty slippers. He shifted from one foot to the other, alarmed to find his hand shaking as he tried to point commandingly to the door.

"You will do no such thing," the man told him in a voice so deep, and so genuinely commanding, it caused John to stand up straighter, a frisson of energy crackling down his spine. "Sit. We have much to discuss, you and I."

John did as asked, his voice fainter as he offered one last protest. "You've no right to be in my private chambers." Clamping his mouth closed, he swallowed thoughts about making an appointment, about the lateness of the hour, about custom and ritual, about the church. The strange man's posture, tone and very presence told him he'd have none of it.

Wearing a dark suit, white collar and black tie, his shoes shined so that John saw reflections from the television, the man looked like an attorney, or an undertaker. His features, even masked in half shadow, were arresting. Strong, angular jawbones met to form a firm, wide chin; long blade-like nose, and lips managed to be sensual though they were thin.

"You've dreamed of me," the man said. His expression held no animosity, yet his brown eyes glittered with fierce intensity.

A ripple of fear coursed through John's middle. It would do no good to lie. "Yes."

He'd seen him, in those dreams, though that was not possible. He had known his name too. Now it was elusive, having slipped away back into the abyss.

He was young, young and full of brash optimism, his future laid out before him. At his side was a handsome man with sharp features and shaggy brown hair. A man whose presence John felt as if a tether bound them, though they were careful not to touch each other. The time had not yet come when such a thing was accepted on the street, even in Los Angeles, even in the Summer of Love.

They'd met Easter Sunday on the day when the Sun had crossed the celestial equator. The Elysian Park love-in was crowded yet, like stars aligning, or planets drawn into orbits, they'd found each other through the smoke and dancing bodies.

The man's brown eyes, locked to his, had enticed John away from the seminary students there to protest such a pagan display on the day of Jesus Christ's resurrection.

Instead of holding his cross high with the others, John dropped it. He took the man's hand when he offered it to him. He kissed his lips, free for the first time to do so, surrounded by people in love, who had nothing but peace in their hearts for all mankind. Soothed by the man's hands on his body, his mind turned from everything he knew and found a place where only desire lived. And, it was good. It was right.

Days passed and he had not returned to school. Instead, he wandered the streets with his new lover. Soon, they looked like hippies, long hair, shoes worn thin, unshaven faces lit with inner happiness. They found places to touch behind bushes, in parks and alleyways and in dark clubs where other men like them dwelled.

John showed him his scars, and rejoiced when they were kissed and tears were shed over them. He told the man his secret longings and hugged him when they were accepted.

"You're going to dig this place," his lover told him one night, leading him into a club with no name on the door, on a street littered with bottles and needles and razor blades.

John kept his hands at his sides as they walked into a darkened room. Low ceilings pressed on him, and music throbbed. *There's a red house over yonder. That's where my baby stays.*

People sat in burgundy leather booths, and crowded narrow walkways. Some were flower children, some looked to be workers from the nearby city of Hollywood, but some were like none John had ever seen. These were pale of skin, and dark of eye, with drawn features and long elegant fingers. Most wore black clothing but, in the back, in a small area exposed to the night sky, on a patio with a fountain of stone, one of them was naked.

"What is this place?" John whispered, reaching out to clasp his lover's hand as he saw the blood that flowed from the veins of the nude woman into IVs with needles that pierced the sweet blue veins in the delicate crooks of her elbows. Valves were opened and closed. Goblets filled. All around him, people sipped. Some fondled one another openly. Others dipped fingers into the blood and painted their faces or the bodies of others.

"Home, John." His lover smiled, laying a finger to John's lips as if to still the protest bubbling there. The touch, so slight, controlled him, pressed him back until his spine rested on the stone wall surrounding the courtyard, his lover sliding a knee between his thighs, taking his hands and easing them up and over his head as he licked his throat where his pulse throbbed madly.

Still, he saw the ones with blades. He watched as a man made tiny slices into the thigh of another, forming a neat row of cuts that ran all the way down to his ankle. He watched as blood tears wept from the open flesh. He moaned as the blade was tossed away and blood was lapped up, while the one who had been cut cried, gently cradling the cutter's head.

"I've never seen—" he said, his words cut off when his lover's teeth pierced his throat, his hand freeing his cock from his jeans, and stroking it until his blood pulsed there too.

John woke from the dream in the middle of an orgasm and cried himself back to sleep.

"Do you remember?" the Englishman asked, leaning forward to rest his elbows on his knees, a crook of fingers forming a resting place for his firm chin.

"Yes." It was a dream, John thought. A terrible, awful, frightening dream.

"That was only the first. There have been others," the stranger said. Again, he did not ask. He knew.

"Yes," John answered, his throat closing, fear a live thing that rippled through his bloated belly and dug fingers into his lungs.

The girl was crying. "I have to do it. I know it's wrong. I prayed on it like you said, but I can't stop. It's the only thing I feel anymore."

John had heard it all before. The sorrow, the tears, the shameful confession. But this young soul stirred him. He understood her, though he could never admit it. "You've made this a substitute for emotion. A way to feel and a way to control the pain inside, worse than the cuts you make into your body."

"No one will love me, if they see. If they know," she said, sobbing now. The worries of a teenaged girl, unable to see that time would change these things if she let it. Not realizing the cruel words of other children would someday mean nothing to her, as she went about her middle-aged life.

I love you, John thought. But, these words he could not say. Nor could he ease her wounds with fingers that understood or kiss away the blood that poured from cuts she made with a rusty blade so she would know that she was not alone. "You must see the school nurse, as you promised last time. You must continue to pray to God so he might show you the light and the way. And, you must promise me you will call, day or night, should you feel an urge to cut deeper." You are so young, he wanted to say. So full of life. Can't you see the world awaits you, and anything you desire could be yours if only you were not afraid?

"I promise, Father. Thank you!"

"Give thanks to the Lord for he is good," John said, closing his eyes, praying along with the girl that this was true.

"For his mercy endures forever," she replied, like a good little Catholic.

"Do you remember?" the stranger asked, his intense eyes drilling into John's.

"I do." The damp of tears watered his gaze, made the man swim, and his own throat hot.

The girl had not been a dream. She had died that summer, never picking up the phone to call him or anyone else for help.

"Still, there is more." The man reached for John's hand, and held it as tenderly as a lover might, his thumb stroking the paper-thin skin.

John shook his head, but he did not pull away.

"Tell me," the Englishman said.

New York. Another borough. Far from the church. Drawn to the lover he'd met in the park on another coast, in another age. This time, after he'd said Mass, offered the Eucharist. *I say to you, unless you eat the flesh of the Son of Man and drink his blood, you do not have life within you.*

"I can't," John told him, even as bedsprings squeaked beneath them and he tore at the clothing of the one he could never resist.

"You will." Lips found his. Tongues tangled and breath mingled. The world dwindled to this place, this hidden room, where no one but his lover could find him.

This time, after giving himself in an offering, still sore with it, he'd held the blade.

"Cut across, not down. Not too deep, darling," his lover told him as the blade glinted in the candlelight. "Do it slow." His cock was hard again. John licked it. Taste of semen mingled with the metallic tang of the blood he had licked from the row of cuts on his lover's arm.

Without meaning to, he'd made a cross on the man's wrist, earning the admonishment and direction. It reminded him of things he did not wish to think on. He groaned, even as his hips lifted to slide his disobedient flesh through the tightly circled fingers of his lover. Closing his eyes, he spurted, forgetting everything but the pleasure, shuddering as he passed the blade to his friend. "Please, do me now. Make them deep."

"Do you remember?" the Englishman said, softer now, his hand cradling John's cheek as his tears fell.

"I don't want to," John protested, shaking his head, afraid of the man's touch, but more afraid of how much he needed it.

"But you must. It's time."

"The blood is not bad. The cutting is not bad. Jesus forgives all but the man who would call Satan the Lord. Forgive me, Lord, for I have sinned, and sinned and sinned again," John said, on his knees at his bedside.

His pants were around his knees, pooled there. His naked belly smooth from the razor he'd drawn over it. His cock so hard, jutting up to the ceiling, its single eye gazing upon the crucifix over the bed without shame.

Scars, long since healed, ribbed his thighs, and when he came, he rubbed his offering into them like a salve, the way his lover had so long ago.

On his night table sat a long-handled razor. Next to it a

cloth and a needle. When the blood flowed, he would paint it upon himself, until he was pretty again.

"None of it was bad. Not then." The Englishman stood before him, a different light shining in his narrowed eyes.

"It never felt wrong. Not with him." John clutched his robe around himself and tried not to cower in the chair. The light from the television shone above the strange man's head.

"It was never wrong. *You* were."

The man had come to him, so like the girl from many years before. "I don't know why I do it. I like the sting. You can't tell nobody, right?"

"Do you...taste it?" Father Mihalis asked him.

"Fuck! I mean, no, Father. No."

Pity, John thought. "Do not curse in the confessional," he said, hands moving over his rosary.

"Forgive me, Father," the man said, chuckling, not taking this seriously at all.

"Only the Lord can forgive you. Visit the altar dedicated to Our Lady, for one hour, and give thanks for the pardon received. Ask for her help so you may overcome your desires."

Father Mihalis made the sign of the cross and the man was gone, slamming the confessional door before he could say the words that sealed the deal. Ah well, he had other plans for him anyway.

The Englishman waited more patiently than even John. He stood in the spread of John's thighs and looked at his shriveled old cock, once so firm and rampant. In his eyes, John saw acceptance of all he had once been and what he was now.

"I killed him," he said, his voice flat and strange with the admission. As if he didn't care, when he did. He always had cared so much.

"You tricked him into the alley behind the church and slit his throat. You let his blood stain the cobblestones."

John nodded. "He kept coming back! Telling me things. He was a bad person. He hurt people. He didn't love the girls he cut. He poured alcohol on their wounds!"

"He *opened* yours."

"Yes! I missed you," John said, knowing what his logical mind had refused to embrace before.

His lover smiled, for the first time, his thin lips slanting across his face, a slash of a dimple appearing on one cheek.

"He was not the only one."

"*You* were the only one," John said, falling to his knees, kissing the shoe of the man he'd once loved. The only man he'd ever loved.

"And you were *my* only one. I gave to you, of my blood, not so you would spill another's, but so you would learn to live." His lover's hand gently stroked the top of his head.

"You drank my blood." It all came crashing back. The dreams that were not dreams at all. The fangs at his throat, suckling. The cock in his mouth. Real.

"But you turned away. Became...this." The sorrow in his voice made John's tears flow anew, yet now fear had come back too.

His eyes darted to the doorway beyond where his lover stood. He could never make it past him but he had to try.

"What now?" John asked, his voice sounding flat to his ears, old and resigned. He knew what was coming next.

Before his lover, still so impossibly young and handsome,

replied, John sat back on his haunches, grabbing the rosary and cross from where it sat on the table next to his recliner, holding it up before himself like a shield. "Be gone, devil! I cast you out in the name of the Lord!"

The Englishman's eyes glowed with intensity, amusement curving his lips into a grin. He reached out and curled his fingers around the cross, squeezing it so hard the spikes pinning Jesus to the wood burst his flesh. Droplets of blood rained down on the carpet as he snatched the rosary from John's hands.

"It only works if you believe," his lover whispered, sliding a finger wet with blood over John's lips.

God help him, John's tongue darted out. Tasting the blood, he moaned, closing his eyes, tilting his head back and offering his throat as his lover painted his mouth and made him pretty once more.

SISTER BESSIE'S BOYS

Gary Earl Ross

W hen I was ten, just before the start of the Korean War, Reverend Cobb began filling my mother's head with notions that I should attend seminary after high school. "Lucas has the gift," he said—mainly because during his visit to my Sunday school class I had dazzled him with my grasp of the catechism. He might have looked at me differently if he had known I memorized it just to show up my brother and sister, who were part of the confirmation class I was too young to attend.

While my father remained neutral and Matthew and Marcia indifferent, my mother embraced the idea her baby would become a minister. Throughout my teens she did her best to steer me toward pulpit life. We discussed Bible verses and sang together in the choir. We volunteered at a nursing home. It had been a long time, she told me, since our little church sent someone to theology school. "The Lawson boy," she said. "We had a special offering to send him but he left school—and his family left the church—after he got a girl in trouble." Her tone left no doubt damnation awaited me if I shamed myself and my church like the Lawson boy.

I was determined not to "get a girl in trouble." Like most boys, I was self-reliant in the pleasure department, though sometimes I prayed for forgiveness after my self-pollution. During my teens, I had two girlfriends, Yvonne from the choir and later Elise from my senior English class. I had kissed each to the point of arousal. With Elise, whose penny-bright skin was simultaneously cool and hot, I sometimes went past that point, which left a quarter-sized wet spot in my crotch. Embarrassing, yes, but nobody got pregnant. Technically, then, I was a virgin when I headed south to Bible college.

My particular Protestant denomination—which shall remain unnamed here—was like most others in 1950s America. With great emphasis on the inerrancy of Scripture, it tended to the next life, leaving unquestioned and intact the injustices of this one, as a matter of social order. Practically all Christian churches accepted legal racial segregation in the South and *de facto* racial segregation in the rest of the nation as part of God's plan. Many denominations maintained national headquarters and seminaries in major cities, but black seminarians (or colored, as we were then) generally attended less well-endowed Bible schools below the Mason-Dixon Line.

My own school will also remain unnamed, though if you're the type who does historical research on strange stories you'll be able to figure out which one it is. Like most similar institutions, my seminary was in a small, largely black town and had fewer amenities than its all-white counterparts. We had older books, secondhand furniture, and buildings in greater disrepair. And we lacked a dormitory. Young men of color who answered the call (no women were ordained then) rented rooms in the homes of host families, most of whom regularly attended services at the college chapel, where every student delivered his first sermons. The system worked well. It offered seminarians a room and a place at a family table for a modest sum and allowed host families to supplement their own limited incomes. Most hosts were couples with no children, young children, or no teenaged girls. The lone exception was Sister Bessie Samples, whom my advisor's summer letter described as "a prim, pious widow whose late husband served as a seminary dean for fifteen years."

I was assigned to the home of Sister Bessie, a retired nurse from up north who would tolerate no smoking or drinking or inappropriate behavior. Included in the letter was a black-and-white photo of a rambling clapboard structure with three stories and a wraparound porch. "She sounds like an old nun," my father said at dinner that evening. But my mother approved of the placement, saying that my volunteer work at the nursing home would come in handy and I could help Sister Bessie with household chores. I suspected they both really meant the housing arrangement would save me from premature parenthood.

In late August, after a too-long, too-hot train ride—during which I had to change to the colored passenger car once we reached the South—a clanking, bald-tired taxi dropped me at the end of a short street with few houses, in front of Sister Bessie's. My first surprise was the color, light gray instead of the white I'd expected from the snapshot. But having traveled all night, I wanted nothing more than to sprawl across my new bed, even though it was still midafternoon. A suitcase in each hand, I went up the steps and knocked on the wood screen door. Then came my second surprise. A petite, coffee-colored woman in a blue housedress opened the front door. She had a ready smile and glittering eyes beneath a short black perm. She pushed opened the screen and held out her hand and said, "You must be Lucas Jackson. I'm Bessie Samples." For a moment after shaking her hand I just stood there, my picture of a severe church lady and foster grandmother shattered. Mrs. Samples, as I had addressed her, couldn't have been more than a year or two older than my mother. "Call me Sister Bessie," she said. "I'll show you to your room."

I stepped into a semicircular foyer, onto a threadbare rug that might have been brand new in the Wilson administration. The air smelled of dusty curtains, dried paste wax, peeling wallpaper, and cracked upholstery. The house felt too old to be occupied by a woman so young. I thought it more suited to the older man whose stern, bespectacled face stared back at me from several framed photographs on the walls. Though part of me hoped the man was Sister Bessie's father, I knew at once he was her husband.

I followed her up creaking old stairs to the third floor, which had a heavy-looking door on each end of the corridor and one in the middle. "This is the little bathroom," she said, indicating the center door. She pushed it open just enough for me to glimpse a sink, toilet and claw-foot tub. The door on the right led to a small room with rose wallpaper, a three-shelf bookcase, a narrow bed, a student desk against the dormer window, and a large mahogany wardrobe in the far corner. "Sorry there's no closet," Sister Bessie said, "but I think that chifforobe is big enough."

Biting back a smile at the word *chifforobe*—which my mother used and my father said made her sound old—I set down my suitcases. "It'll be fine, ma'am." Then I thanked her for her hospitality.

"I expect you want to rest up," she said. "Come on down for supper about six-thirty. Then we can go over the house rules."

Supper consisted of corn, baked squash, collard greens, potatoes and the best fried chicken I'd tasted since my grandmother died. As we ate, she recited the house rules in a soft voice that belied the seriousness in her luminous brown eyes: no smoking, drinking or female visitors—but classmates were welcome to join me in the parlor for chess or checkers or one of the board games her husband had collected. "Walter used to say the Lord's work demands a mind at peace with itself, and games are a good way to settle the brain." She nodded toward another picture of the man I'd seen in the foyer, and I found it hard to picture them together as husband and wife. I couldn't imagine why she'd want such a face looking at her in almost every room.

I blinked and returned my attention to her just as she was explaining that supper was at six-thirty every night except on those days she might be delayed at Dr. Bledsoe's office. Hiram Bledsoe, she explained, was the only colored physician in the region, with an office almost fifty miles away. Though she had retired from nursing, four or five times a month she made the drive to his office to help out. He paid her a small stipend for her services and kept her well supplied with basic medicines so she could treat the sick in her own town. Whenever she was late returning from Dr. Bledsoe's, I was to cook my own dinner or make a sandwich.

I had to be in by ten each night. "Most likely you'll be in before then 'cause there's not much to do in this town." I was responsible for cleaning my own room and the bathroom beside it, as well as washing dishes and helping her with yard work. She did laundry every Monday, but I had to carry my hamper down to the first-floor laundry room. I had unlimited access to every room in the house except, of course, her second floor bedroom and bath and the third floor storage room at the opposite end of the hall. The books in her husband's first-floor study might be of particular interest. "Many aren't in the seminary library, which gives you a leg up on your classmates." If my studies were done for the day, I could watch one of the two television stations any evening of the week except Saturday or Sunday, but I was welcome to join her those nights for "Gunsmoke" and "Ed Sullivan." She seldom listened to radio dramas anymore, so I could take the tabletop model in the parlor up to my room but I must keep the volume low. Then she asked if I had any questions. When I shook my head, she smiled and patted my hand, which gave me a tiny electric jolt.

I remembered the shock in bed that night and thought of her pleasant face and wide smile. Deciding she was pretty for an older woman, I reached for myself. But I stopped before finishing, partly because I was uneasy about staining sheets she would launder and partly because I had a fleeting thought that Walter might be staring at me from beyond the unfamiliar walls. If I was going to resume the habit that had been such a struggle for me, I'd have to invest in Kleenex and decorate the room to make it my own.

We settled into a workable routine quickly and easily. I rose each morning at seven, by which time Sister Bessie had gathered eggs from the chicken coop she kept out back and made breakfast. By seven-thirty, her husband's black lunch pail in hand, I was out the door for the two-mile walk to the seminary, where class began at eight-thirty. By four-thirty or five I was climbing the front porch steps, prepared to study or undertake whatever chores my hostess wanted done before supper. After washing and drying the dishes, I spent an hour or two studying in my room, which I had personalized by shelving my few books and putting family pictures atop the bookcase. Sometimes while I washed the dishes, Sister Bessie would receive a visitor she took into Walter's study. In my first month I saw a mother with a child who looked sick and a woman whose abdomen was so large it seemed she might have the baby right there. (The telephone on a small table at the foot of the stairs jangled a few nights later, and Sister Bessie left to deliver that baby.) A few times the visitor she escorted into the study was a healthy-looking girl or young woman whose face was taut with worry. These she always drove home herself, later.

A couple of times a week I watched something on television but was always in bed by ten, except when I joined Sister Bessie for "Gunsmoke" on Saturday night. On Sunday, in her blue Pontiac, she drove us both to services at the seminary chapel, where I sat with my classmates while she took her place in the pew dedicated to Walter's memory. On Sunday evening we added "Alfred Hitchcock Presents" to our viewing. Sometimes at night, especially after we had watched something together, I would lie alone in bed picturing the light in her eyes and the softness of her skin and imagining the music of her voice. Pictures of my parents and siblings having helped push Walter into the background, I would relieve myself. I always put the wad of Kleenex into a pocket of the trousers I would wear the next day so I could dispose of the evidence after I left. My vague shame aside, those first weeks passed with a comfort I hoped would stretch through four years of study.

Then everything changed.

One afternoon in late October I came home to find Sister Bessie seated in her rocker in the half-darkened parlor, gazing at the windows as if she could see through the thick curtains. Wearing a black dress I'd never seen, she kept her hands in her lap. The tail of a wrinkled white handkerchief stuck out of one fist and a framed photo of Walter was clutched in the other. She turned to me when I asked if she was all right, and the tears on her cheeks glistened. "Walter died today," she whispered, wiping her eyes. "Five years ago today. I always have trouble getting through this night."

"I understand." I perched on the edge of the armchair across from her and gently took the photo. I sat back, studied it. The first time I had seen Walter, I had been surprised at how old he looked—white hair, pouched eyes—and calculated he must have been at least twenty-five years his wife's senior. Now I saw the firmness of his jaw, the precision with which he trimmed his mustache and thick brows, the knowing kindness behind the horn-rimmed glasses. "You must miss him. Everybody at school says he was a great man."

"He was," she said, "and a wonderful husband." I handed back the photo. Then she told me about the Reverend Walter Samples, the man whose face I couldn't walk five paces without seeing. They had met when he was a visiting pastor at a small church in Harlem. She herself had belonged to another church but had been one of the registered nurses at a small colored hospital who cared for him after an emergency appendectomy. "He was gentle and kind and never complained about pain. But there was sadness in him beyond pain. You see, his wife had died in childbirth a year earlier, with the baby stillborn. Walter had this energy that demanded you pay attention to him, a strength that needed to be shared with more than church folk. But he was all alone. I had no parents, no real friends..." Their courtship had been brief, and she had been with him for two postings before he got the call to the seminary. They'd had twenty happy years together. "My biggest regret," she said, "is that I never gave him the child he wanted."

I never felt more drawn to her, more aroused, than I did that afternoon. I ached to hold her, to help her ease the pain. I imagined myself brushing her hair aside, pressing my lips to her forehead as I whispered reassurances, trailing kisses down her cheek. But I dared not cross the line that stretched between us. I made dinner for her instead—hamburgers, peas, fried potatoes. Afterward, she went upstairs early, and I, unable to study, spent the evening in front of the television, from "Phil Silvers" right through "Red Skelton." At ten I climbed the stairs to my room, surprised to see light below the door of the third floor storage room and to hear the periodic sniffle of someone fighting back tears. With Bessie back in my mind, I went into my room determined to discharge my desire with Vaseline and Kleenex. But my attempt was half-hearted in the wake of her grief and I gave up because I felt cheap and dirty for wanting a woman still crying for her dead husband. I fell asleep thinking of her, which is why, later, when I stirred at the sound of my door opening, I thought I might be dreaming.

Before reason could settle into my waking brain, Sister Bessie slipped into bed beside me, and my breath caught. "I don't mean to startle you, Lucas," she whispered, as if there were someone else in the house to hear. "I just need to feel somebody warm next to me tonight." She turned away from me, easing her back against me and pulling my right arm over her stomach. "Thank you for letting me ramble on about Walter. You're very sweet."

I was too terrified to move, but my body reacted to her nevertheless. Even with my cotton pajamas and her flannel nightgown between us, the cleft of her buttocks was a perfect nesting place for my yet-untested manhood. I thickened almost instantly, feeling the pressure of her nearness become a sweet tingling in my belly and balls. My heart slammed against the wall of my chest and I swallowed again and again. Still I dared not move because I did not want to disrespect her, to misunderstand what she intended by coming into my bed. After a minute or two she released my arm and reached behind herself to touch me through my pajama bottom. Her fingers were long and thin and unbuttoned the opening with no trouble. They wriggled inside and took hold, a single fingernail gently scratching my scrotum and her thumb making circles in the mat of my pubic hair. She guided my painfully hard penis through the opening and whispered, "Lift my gown." I obeyed, and she raised herself enough to let the flannel be drawn above her hips. Then she raised her right leg and locked it behind me, drawing me against her and into a warmth and wetness ever so much better than my hand. Almost disbelieving that I was at last losing my virginity, I sank deep inside her and shuddered. She began to grind against me, moaning softly, pulling me into her and relaxing enough to let me slide back, probably only four or five times before I spilled into her years of fantasy and fear—Yvonne and Elise and getting a girl in trouble. "Don't stop," she breathed. "You're young. You can get hard again." And I did.

I slept soundly that night, stirring only once sometime after three when I thought I heard something like creaking floorboards. But Bessie was still curled against me, breathing easily, holding my fingers against her belly with both hands—and I slipped back into sleep without fully emerging from it.

When I woke the next morning I was alone. For a moment I entertained the idea it had all been a dream born of desire so intense it had erased the line between the real and the unreal.

But when I slid out of bed to use the bathroom I could not deny the crust on the sheet that flaked beneath my fingertips or the whitish residue that ringed the head of my penis. The realization that finally I'd experienced sex so overwhelmed me I needed to steady myself by gripping the pedestal sink with one hand as I used the other to guide my pee into the toilet. My flash of pride was replaced by a rush of shame for having taken advantage of Sister Bessie's grief. Not only was she somewhere around my mother's age, we'd had sex outside of marriage. I had been raised to believe fornication was wrong. Now the prospect of facing her in the morning light made me dawdle over washing and dressing.

As I left my room to go down for breakfast, I noticed the storage room door was ajar. I pushed it open quietly—only to find it too dim to see inside—and turned on the light.

The layout was the mirror image of my own room, but the similarity stopped there. The curtains over the dormer were faded from sunlight and discolored with dust. On the dresser lay a wallet, fountain pen, gold pocket watch, gold cross, and Bible with a cracked binding. Men's shoes—five or six pairs— were lined up against the baseboard of the far wall. The walls held pictures of Walter and certificates that bore his name. The largest photograph was flanked by two wall sconces with melted-down white candles not dusty enough to have been in the room as long as everything else. On a hook near one of the sconces hung the black dress Bessie had worn the previous day, and I wondered if she had stretched out naked on this bed beside the layers of men's clothing it held. Atop the pile was a black clerical suit with an unsnapped white collar, laid out as if the body inside had simply disappeared. But the disappearance felt recent, for as I stood inhaling shoe leather and fabric and dust I realized I had smelled Walter on his widow in my bed.

Shaking, I switched off the light and closed the door as quietly as I had opened it. I returned to the bathroom, to wash the smell of the tomb off my hands and out of my nose. Then I went down to breakfast late, afraid to meet Sister Bessie's gaze but ever conscious of Walter's scrutiny as I passed every picture of him from the second floor to the kitchen.

She set the plate of eggs, toast and sausage in front of me as if nothing had happened, then stepped back and smoothed her yellow housedress. "We need to talk."

Still afraid to look up at her, I mumbled some kind of apology about last night. "I didn't mean to...to..."

"Felt like you meant it," she said. "And it would hurt my feelings if you didn't."

"But what we did...it was a..." I wanted to use the word *sin* but couldn't bring myself to say it to the minister's widow who'd taken my virginity while maintaining a museum exhibit. "All my fault," I said, certain I was apologizing to both of them.

She took a step forward and lifted my chin so that I had to look into her eyes. She was smiling. "There's no fault here," she said quietly. "It was what I wanted to happen. It was a kindness, a precious kindness that meant more to me than you'll ever know."

"But I thought..."

She shook her head. "You're here to learn how to be a minister to people, real people with real problems and real flaws. What we did last night is something real people do. If you don't understand that, you'll be useless to any congregation you serve." She released my chin and said, "Now eat up and get going. You'll be late." Moving to the stove, she began to dish up her own breakfast. "We'll talk tonight and I'll tell you what Walter would have said about last night."

Thus began my parallel education in the ways of the flesh. I couldn't have imagined then—as I fumbled through my day, forgetting where I was supposed to be and half paying attention when I got there—how much that education would shape me into the man I have become. I know only that all morning and all afternoon I thought about Sister Bessie and what I'd discovered. Walter had stared at me from so many photographs I imagined him taking shape inside the clothes on the bed, willing himself back into bodily form to point his finger at the wretched sinner now sleeping in his house. But I thought also about the foot Sister Bessie hooked over my calf and the firmness of her backside pressed against me, of the stiffness of her nipples when she guided my hand to them and the three times I slid inside her and exploded. Despite my uncertainty and despite Walter, I couldn't wait to get home.

For supper we had pork chops, string beans, fried green tomatoes and cornbread. At Sister Bessie's request, I said grace, stumbling over words that had spilled out of me with automatic precision since the age of seven. When I finished, she said, "Amen," and began what would have been our customary how-was-your-day small talk. My recounting of the day's trivia was as awkward as my blessing of the food. Sister Bessie set down her fork and looked at me, and I mumbled through a mouthful of cornbread that everything was delicious.

"All right," she said. "Last night we did it. We had sex. We made love." She drew in a deep breath. "We fucked."

I flinched and forced down the cornbread before my throat could close and choke me.

Bessie reached across the table and placed her right hand

over my left. It was warm and soft but firm enough to hold mine in place. "That doesn't give you the right to treat me like I have the plague." She squeezed my wrist until I looked up at her. "Or to cast the first stone."

"I'm sorry," I said. "I'm…" I almost said, *I'm not Walter* but caught myself. "I don't know what I am…except confused."

"Then let's talk about your confusion." She released my hand and sat back. "Are you afraid you're a sinner and going to hell?"

I nodded.

"We're all sinners," she said. "We can't help it. It's how we're born, who we are. But the forgiveness of sin is perpetual. Walter believed that."

"I don't understand."

She sat forward again, her eyes alight. "God is good, right? They teach you that."

I nodded.

"Why would a good God send a young man like you to hell?"

"Because I'm a sinner!" I felt my own eyes welling.

"No matter what they tell you, sin is relative," she said. "Is what we did worse than what Hitler did? Suppose he got a chance to repent and go to heaven while all the people he had murdered never got that chance and went to hell. Does that sound fair? Does that sound like something a good God would allow?"

"But I…I've wronged *you*."

"How? Did you steal from me? Hurt me or kill me? No. Legally, you're a grown man who did something grown men do." She smiled. "Did you bear false witness against me?"

"I didn't tell a soul," I said.

"I said *false* witness. But why wouldn't you tell something that was true?"

"Because...because it felt...private...between you and me and..."

"And because you liked it."

I felt my cheeks go hot. "Yes."

"It *was* private, between us and God, and we both liked it. Walter believed everybody is forgiven, except for the worst sinners, killers and those who hurt others, willfully and repeatedly. And because we live in a world where some folks are so afraid of pleasure they can't dance or play, he was never free to say so, but he didn't believe in hell either."

My stomach clenched. The great man whose gaze glowed hellfire didn't believe in a central tenet of our faith. I didn't ask my next question because she saw it in my face.

"Walter believed the worst sinners could never find grace beside God and would simply enter limbo, an eternal nothingness and not an inferno, because a good God wouldn't create hell." She reached across the table again, with both hands this time, and took hold of mine. "A good God would want ministers who didn't judge but simply did their best to help. A good God would create ways men and women could find comfort and strength with each other to let them face their days with hope. My husband believed in joy and I have kept that part of him as close to me as I can."

After dinner she went upstairs while I washed the dishes. As I dried and shelved them, I could hear water filling the tub in the large second floor bathroom. Ordinarily, I'd have gone up to my room to begin my evening study, but I was too agitated to do so just then and did not want to risk seeing her in her robe as I went from the second to the third floor. I decided to wait until

I heard her get into the tub. But the sound of her feet sliding along the tub bottom as she lowered herself into water—something I'd heard before—did not come. Instead, she called down and asked if I would come up. I closed my eyes for a moment, then mounted the stairs.

The bathroom door was wide open. She stood inside, on the rug beside the steaming tub, naked and shimmering in the light of votive candles on the sink and windowsill.

Occasionally I had seen my mother's back or too much leg or her whole body moving past me in only a bra and slip. Once or twice I had burst into my sister Marcia's room to share something urgent, only to find her half-dressed and screaming at me. But until this moment, I had never before, not even in a magazine, seen a naked woman. I couldn't help gaping.

"Come in and close the door," she said. "I'm cold."

I did so, my back against the door and one hand on the knob, though I couldn't have run if I wanted to. I stared at her candlelight-dappled body, my heart in my throat. For what felt like a full minute neither of us said anything. She had skin the color of ginger, long thin arms, round hips, and dark-nippled breasts large enough to fill a hand but too small to sag. The dark hair at the apex of her legs had been shaped into a palm-sized triangle. A whitish arc of a scar was on her inner left thigh—a childhood bicycle accident, I learned later. Her feet were small, with pinky toes curled almost out of sight. When I looked up at her face, Bessie Samples was smiling. She stepped forward and began to unbutton my shirt, and I swallowed, hard.

"We're going to take a bath together," she said, "because sometimes that's what lovers do." She stood on tiptoes to kiss me—our first kiss—and her warm lips drew my tongue into her mouth. She sucked it gently, scraping it with her own, then released me and let her heels return to the floor. "Afterward we'll go to my room and leave the lights on so we can see every bit of each other." She opened my shirt and peeled it off my arms, then pulled my undershirt over my head. "We'll make love, joyfully, without shame." Pressing her face to my chest, she licked first one nipple and then the other. "One day I'll trim the hair around these and you'll feel it more when I touch them." Her fingers undid my belt, unzipped my trousers. "I'll touch you in ways and places you never thought of, and I'll show you how to do the same to me." Her hand freed my now-throbbing penis from my boxers. "I'll teach you everything Walter taught me." She sat on the edge of the tub and leaned toward me, swirling her tongue around the edge of my penis and taking me into her mouth for several heartbeats during which all thoughts of Walter melted away. Standing, she pushed my trousers down, and I stepped out of my shoes. "We will be lovers," she whispered, "and we will talk and laugh and learn all about each other and find the most exquisite happiness God offers. We will be lovers but we will never be *in* love. You must never tell me you love me because you must save that for the woman who carries your children, a woman who will love you in return because you will bring her a joy most other men can't." She steadied me as I pulled off my socks. "We will never be *in* love because I am too old for you, because you could never be the minister you need to be if scandal hangs over your head."

"What if I don't want to be a minister anymore?"

"It is your calling," she said, stepping into the tub first and holding my hand as I stepped in after her. "You can help so many replace their fear of God with a love of life. You can bring so many out of the shadows."

As we sank into hot water together, I no longer cared if Walter was looking.

That was the first step on my journey out of the shadows of fear and into the light of possibility. For the next four years, by day I studied the history, prophets and philosophy of Judaism and Christianity. I studied Greek, Latin, Hebrew and Aramaic. I read early English translations of the Old and New Testaments and the Apocrypha, as well as books about the Hampton Court Conference that resulted in the King James Bible. I read the *Annals* of Tacitus, which documented our faith with a brief notation of the crucifixion of "Christus." I pored over maps of the Holy Land and traced the rise of Christianity from Catholicism to the Reformation. Along the way I met not only the holy men and women of the Bible but also Constantine, various popes, Luther, Calvin and the thinkers who had influenced the many paths of the cross. I studied ethics, pastoral counseling, the sacraments, homiletics and ecumenism. I excelled at my course work.

In the evening I discussed what I had learned with Sister Bessie, sometimes at the supper table, sometimes in the parlor over coffee or when she was teaching me to dance, sometimes in bed. Even when one of us was sick and the other brought up chicken soup and medicine, we talked endlessly. I learned to listen and think. We had spirited debates that sometimes led us naked past Walter's pictures and into his study, where Sister Bessie pulled down books and monographs that explored topics not mentioned at the seminary: popes who had fathered children and committed murders, nuns in convents beside monasteries who had buried in the walls the babies of their unsanctioned affairs, the bloody atrocities of the Crusades, devout reformers who thought the retarded were possessed and attempted to beat the devil out of them, European scholars and Southern ministers who all produced books and tracts that "proved" only whites had souls. She gave me these, she said, so I would never forget that "In the end, everybody is hopelessly human."

And at night I slept in her arms, or she in mine, after passionate lovemaking that was ever a revelation. It was she who taught me how to touch and be touched, how to catch a nipple between my teeth without causing pain, how to produce shivers with a fingernail in the shallow pocket behind the knee. Together we explored virtually every possible position for intercourse—in my bed and hers, on the floor and the stairs and the davenport in the parlor and two or three times with me standing between her legs as she lay back on the kitchen table. Hers was the first woman's orgasm I saw (self-induced), the first finger to penetrate me, the first mouth to clamp onto me and let me spend down her throat. I trusted her enough to let her blindfold me or tie my hands to the bed or drip hot candle wax onto my back. The third time she held my ears and steered my face between her legs, she whispered, "Don't just lick me. Suck me. Kiss me. Inhale me and learn to love the smell." And I complied, my erection so hard I thought my skin would split.

I set foot in what I'd come to think of as Walter's room only once more, the weekend before the start of my sophomore year. Having returned early to end my summer celibacy before classes started, I found myself alone in the house that first Friday while Sister Bessie worked at Dr. Bledsoe's. The room had changed considerably. The walls still carried photos and certificates but the clothes and shoes and personal effects were gone. The curtains were newer and translucent enough that the room seemed more lighted shrine than mausoleum. Walter was here but I could no longer smell him.

Later, as I moved through the house, I began to see his pictures differently. What had struck me at first as severity now seemed intense contemplation and perceptive wisdom.

I told Sister Bessie I loved her only once, as we walked home from the chapel after my final graded sermon for homiletics, near the end of my final year. Before she could begin her speech, I smiled and said, "This isn't a marriage proposal. I'm just trying to say thank you." The last time we made love was early in the morning before I drove to pick up my parents at the train station for my afternoon graduation. Straddling me, her fingertips gliding through my thickening chest hair, she whispered, "I love you too and always will."

We wrote to each other off and on for years. She congratulated me on each of my postings to inner city churches in various parts of the country and offered helpful insights on congregation politics. She came to my wedding four years after graduation and told me she thought Janet was a wonderful choice. She even traveled for the baptisms of our three children. Bessie remained a friend for the rest of her life, and when she passed away, nearly thirty years later, I flew south to attend her funeral.

A special pew was set aside for Sister Bessie's boys, six of us who had roomed with her during our seminary days. Six black reverends, all strangers to each other and about four years apart in age, all but one younger than I. Four of us looked at the others with more than apparent wonder and the remaining two stared straight ahead, but no one asked the questions I am sure some of us were pondering: How many of us had known with her a more than maternal love? Who among us had thought we were the only one she had loved into better manhood? Perhaps it was the sin of pride, but one line of questioning I believed was mine alone: Was I the first? Had I inspired the change in Walter's room and perhaps a change in her? As she was lowered into the ground beside Walter, I cried for the wisest, most passionate woman I had ever known—and for the ghost who had shaped her as surely as she had shaped me.

Though this document will remain sealed until fifty years after my own death, this story would have ended with that funeral so many years ago if not for the recent razing of the Samples house, which had passed through several hands since Bessie's death. Construction workers preparing to lay the foundation for a new elementary school unearthed in the yard something that sickened them and drew the national press. At first the four fetal skeletons inside small wooden boxes led to public speculation that the former nurse had run a secret abortion clinic in the days before *Roe v. Wade.* Tabloid headlines like *Southern Abortion Horror* and *Fetal Graveyard* brought to mind the worried-looking young women I had seen her lead into Walter's study so long ago. Hungry reporters crawled through her life with maddening persistence. Two or three tried to get in touch with me, but I declined every interview request and never saw a disclosure from any of Bessie's boys. Later, when matrilineal DNA tests confirmed the fetuses were siblings, a medical examiner concluded Bessie had handled her own miscarriages, and the story died a quiet death.

Sometimes I wonder about those miscarriages. Had she had them during her marriage, or had the found four been sired by one or more of Bessie's boys? Looking in the mirror at a man who is heavier, wrinkled, bespectacled, white-haired and too often so serious he looks more like Walter than he'd care to admit, I wonder if I did get someone in trouble after all. But I seldom linger on such thoughts—or on whether she ended the pregnancies of desperate girls and buried those remains where they will never be found. I am happy with my own life, with my wife and children and the congregants who seek my counsel and trust me with their deepest secrets, even in my retirement. You see, after nearly fifty years of marriage, and the requisite back pain and stiff joints, I still give Janet a shattering orgasm or two every time we make love. She still licks me into a harder erection than my age should allow, and we grapple with an abandon that sometimes steals sleep from our visiting grandchildren. At such times I know that part of Sister Bessie still lives inside me, in the profound gift she has given me—a mind and a life at peace with themselves. The part of her that sleeps deserves an eternal rest undisturbed by my curiosity.

REYNOLDS'S TALE

Adrian Ludens

It has been written that there are secrets that should never be shared. I am in partial agreement with this assessment. Men and women die daily and nightly, guilt gnawing away at their resolve to live. The thread of their long-kept secret steadfastly unravels the fabric of their mortal coil until they no longer have a tether to this earthly realm. Up these thoughts must drift into the endless inverted abyss. But what if the dreaded secret were revealed at a time not inopportune? Could one's conscience be eased and death staved off? Perhaps. I have two secrets. I shall endeavor to share one of them, lightening the burden that I bear and thus extending—I fervently hope—my life. I only ask that you hear my tale and judge me not.

Call me Reynolds. A few years ago, on the second of October 1849, to be precise, I sat at a large bow-window of a coffee house in Baltimore. For some weeks I had been in ill health. My body endured the challenges associated with an extended illness, while my mind underwent certain changes. But now I found my strength returning in unprecedented abundance. So also, joie de vivre enveloped me. A happy and inquisitive mood enveloped me. I rushed headlong into each new day with an alacrity and curiosity heretofore unknown to my personality.

With a newspaper still folded on my knee and a fine cigar hanging idly from my lips, I found myself continuously distracted by those who bustled along the dirty street below the window. The street, being one of Baltimore's principal thoroughfares, was crowded with humanity. As the lengthening shadows assimilated into the growing darkness that comes with the retreat of the sun, the tumultuous sea of faces below filled my mind with a hundred flights of fancy. I gave up completely on my paper and cigar. My coffee grew cold. I became absorbed in contemplation of the ever-changing scene below me.

At first my observations were random in nature. My eyes would fall upon a face, or perhaps only a single feature—a woman's nose, for instance—and with a preternatural clarity, I could know everything I cared to about that person. I noted at a glance the birds of a feather. I mentally sequestered groups of noblemen, merchants, tradesmen, clerks, gamblers, lunatics, pickpockets, drunkards, murderers, clergymen and lawyers. Each aforementioned grouping descended in the scale of what could only be termed gentility. Deeper and darker character studies presented themselves for my speculation.

As the night deepened, so also my interest in the ebb and flow of humanity below me deepened. The character of the crowd altered, growing more sinister and more decadent. Ruffians seethed and searched for violence by swaggering down the center of the thoroughfare. Heavily painted women of the night kept to the shadows and attempted to seduce and beguile with toothless, slack-jawed smiles. The rays of the gas lamps spotlighted many interesting visages. The sight of a legless man rolling himself along on a small, wheeled cart brought forth in me a smile so broad that I felt my dry bottom lip split. I relished the discomfort.

Then a pickpocket misjudged his mark and the intended victim clamped down on the miscreant's wrist and drew him in close. The mark used a grimy thumb to gouge the shifty fellow's right eye out. The pickpocket howled and the crowd parted around them, but never stopped moving. The intended victim's lips moved and I interpreted his words clearly. "How'd ya like it? Me taking sumthin' from you? Now ya knows how it feels!" The pickpocket scurried up the street, his hand cupped to his empty socket. The angry man held a pose reminiscent of Jack Horner for a few moments. Then, apparently realizing this "plum" on his thumb could lead to unwanted attention, he shook it loose and hastened away in the opposite direction.

I stifled a titter and, taken aback, wondered why the events I had witnessed caused this reaction within me. My eyes skipped over the throng when there came into my view a countenance so forlorn—so *haunted*—that I lost interest in all else. His presence among the throng was like that of an exotic fish among a school of carp. I pressed my brow to the glass and scrutinized the object of my instant fascination.

The man was short in stature, and quite thin. A shock of hair the color of raven's feathers contrasted with his waxy-white face. A mustache perched atop lips that twisted in a petulant frown. A broad forehead and prominent nose lent strength to his features. Conversely, the deep hollows beneath and the furrowed brows above the stranger's eyes revealed a profoundly troubled heart. But his eyes held the most damning evidence. From only the briefest of glances, I felt as if I experienced firsthand his vast mental capability, his excessive terror, his fervent desire to love and be loved, his avarice, his hopefulness, his overwhelming guilt and his supreme despair. He disappeared for a moment, lost in the waves of filthy, ragged humanity. I readjusted my gaze and found my own reflection in the glass. An overwhelming interest in the stranger pressed me into motion. I threw a few coins on the table, put on my overcoat and seized my hat and cane. I made my way onto the street and pushed through the crowd in the direction I'd seen the haunted-looking man take. With only slight difficulty, I found him among the throng and fell in about twenty paces back.

A thick fog, refracting the rays of the gas lamps, illuminated the scene with a garish luster. I followed my quarry and gradually closed the distance between us. His clothes were shabby. He hunched his shoulders against the clamminess of the night. Never once did he turn his head to look back. By and by he passed an alley and I seized the opportunity to speak with him in a semiprivate environment.

I lunged forward, grasped his right arm just above the elbow and pulled him into the alley. My quarry thrashed and struggled to free himself. "Unhand me!" he shrilled.

I spun him so that we faced each other. "I shall, but do not flee. I have friendly intentions and wish only for a moment of intelligent conversation." Our eyes locked and after a moment's hesitation, the stranger gave me a brief nod. I released his arm and he waited with countenance guarded and mistrustful.

"Who are you and what business would you have with me?" he asked.

"Call me Reynolds. When I saw you on the street, I first mistook you for a long-lost friend." The lie would do him no harm. "I drew close enough that my error became apparent. I realized that I would not rekindle an old friendship on this night after all, but thought perhaps I could forge a new one instead." I lifted my inflection and turned the statement into a question.

The despair so prevalent in his deep brown eyes gave way to a spark of hope. I fanned the flame with an encouraging smile to which he tentatively responded. "Do tell me," I invited. "What your name is, good sir, and what is your trade?"

A giddy, mad gleam came into his eyes. "I am Poe. I am a writer." This time he seized *my* arm and steered me deeper into the alley. We strode between tall, worm-eaten tenements that leaned over us as if they would topple at any moment. Our path wound in random directions and my new friend spoke rapidly and with vehemence as we trudged along the crooked paving stones and rankly growing grass.

"I write, but I must censor myself at every turn. It is my most fervent desire to write about love. But—" he broke off and shuddered. "The love I feel—the love I believe in—cannot be discussed rationally or with intelligence in general company without threat of persecution. I am a *vox clamantis in deserto*, a voice crying in the wilderness. Inside my chest beats the heart of a romantic. I laugh, I cry, I love with reckless abandon."

I nodded my encouragement and Poe continued.

"For instance, some years ago I had intended to write a love story about an old man and his live-in companion. I had the first line of the story written: 'I loved the old man.' Yet I knew such a tale would never sell, would only ruin me. My own inner fears preyed upon me and twisted my original intentions into an abomination. What started as a story about love had devolved into one of murder, guilt and madness.

"In another tale, I intended one character, Valdemar by name, to reveal his love for a colleague while under the influence of hypnosis. I included in the first draft a scene of passionate lovemaking between Valdemar and my narrator. My body and soul were alight with desire as I wrote, but upon completion I took the pages and hid them away."

Poe's voice cracked with emotion at this revelation. I put one arm around his shoulder in a gesture of consolation. We did our best to ignore the filth that festered around the dammed-up gutters. The overall atmosphere around me, including the author himself, conveyed nothing but desolation.

"Every story or poem I have ever written started out vastly different. But always the evil creeps back into my heart and into my work. My corrupt revisions are of death, sorrow, loneliness and madness! Why must it be that way? I have become my own worst enemy. My works, upon my rereading of them, rear up and spit in my face!

"The treasure-seeker and his servant in 'The Gold Bug' were meant to be lovers! Another of my characters, Roderick Usher, buried his sister alive in the published version of his tale. My original draft pitted Roderick and his sister in a precocious battle for the affections of the unnamed narrator. Oh, the adventures in lovemaking they shared!"

My new acquaintance seemed far away for a moment, placing himself in the story, perhaps. Then his shoulders sagged and his eyes once again took on their defeated, yet defiant, cast. "That manuscript and so many others molder in a locked box somewhere. I couldn't bear to burn them, nor could I allow them to be discovered by prying, judgmental eyes."

Our pace had slowed. We turned a corner and a blaze of light burst upon our view. We stood before a temple erected for the purpose of whiskey and gin worship. A tattered sign next to the entrance advertised upstairs rooms for rent BY HOUR OR BY NIGHT.

Poe spun to face me. "Do you know that in my original version of 'The Cask of Amontillado,' the hole left in the wall was not at eye-level but instead was positioned parallel with Fortunato's waist? Montresor forgave him, you see. Only wanted to tease him, ply him with drink, and then tear down the wall between them so that they might abandon themselves to their desires in privacy. But my practical side got the better of me, and the story now is one of cruel revenge."

He stepped forward and seized the lapels of my overcoat. "William Wilson only ran from his own desires! The revelers in what became 'The Masque of the Red Death' were meant to indulge in a night of freedom and self-discovery. I changed the stories only because I needed money for food and lodging!"

A clock struck eleven. The author gazed into my eyes imploringly. "Is it too late? Can I repent of past mistakes and seize salvation at this both literal and figurative eleventh hour?"

I looked down into Poe's eyes and could find no fault in him. His wants, needs and desires, so long buried and hidden, could still be tended to, fertilized and brought to fruition. Though I had no particular attraction to men in general, I felt I could help this unfortunate fellow achieve some small measure of happiness. Thus, I navigated the creaking, rotten stairs to the entrance and once inside, inquired about securing a room.

Poe visibly trembled as we ascended the stairs. With the door closed and the begrimed key turned in the lock, my companion fell upon me with fervent kisses. Never before had I felt so *needed* by anyone. We removed our garments rather ceremoniously and stood before a grimy looking-glass. I nuzzled his neck and cupped one hand on his heart, which beat like that of a frightened captive bird. Of the haunted look that had dominated his visage there was no trace. At length, we fell together onto the bed.

The bookish fellow proved to be an attentive lover. I did my best to impress upon him my appreciation and repay him for his efforts. Poe's kisses left on my lips a pine-needle flavor; evidence of time spent in the gin mills. I kissed and licked my way down his spine, eliciting shivers unlike those he brought about in his readers. But when I caressed his buttocks with my erect manhood, Poe cast an anxious look over his shoulder. The brooding, tortured soul had returned and I decided instantly not to welcome it. Instead, I bounded across the room and removed the grimy looking-glass from its place. I tossed it on the mattress and maneuvered Poe into position over the mirror. His physical arousal still evident, I knew I had only to contend with his mental reservations. Using my own saliva to facilitate our congress, I pressed myself forward until we were one. Then, as I caressed his shoulders, neck and back with my fingertips I exhorted him, saying: "Cast aside the shackles that bind you! Look inside yourself. Love yourself!" He groaned and rocked in a rhythm that complimented mine. Tentatively at first, and then increasing in passion and intensity, we moved until I felt my own climax approaching. I let one hand slide across his hip, intending to pleasure his member, but stopped short. I confess I gasped at the serendipitous event I witnessed. Poe was weeping, not with sorrow, but with joy, as if the rusted chains that choked his soul had been shattered. As his tears pattered onto the glass, he bent, and tasted them with the tip of his tongue. I watched Poe press his lips to the glass; his reflection returned the kiss. It was the most beautiful thing I'd ever witnessed.

In the end, we lay exhausted and tangled in the dingy sheets. As the pale gray of dawn crept upon the city, Poe began to twitch and show signs of growing unease. I inquired what troubled him.

"It cannot be this way. I cannot allow it." He sat up and pulled a sheet to his waist, as if suddenly ashamed. Feelings of confusion and frustration welled up within me. I could not fathom why one would deny happiness and forsake love, instead turning and running headlong into despair and loneliness. I told him as much.

"You can't begin to understand! Have you no fear of discovery? No fear of derision, loathing and ruin?"

I did not, and I admitted as much. It was then, in my attempt to soothe his misgivings, that I made my most horrific mistake. It was an error of judgment I deeply regret to this day. But how could I guess the outcome? My illness and accompanying fever had changed me, as I have already indicated. And, not knowing what result my words would have, I told the tormented little author my secret.

"Last year, I spent several weeks among an ostracized tribe from one of the Greater Antillean islands," I revealed. "While I was living with the tribe, they introduced me to an act of depravity so taboo I dare not say it aloud. Yet the desire to perform the act has sunk hooks of addiction into me. I am a slave to it in body and mind. You needn't feel guilt, my friend. There is no comparison. For my most pleasurable experiences were..."

I cupped one hand to Poe's ear and revealed my most cherished act. His eyes dilated as I described the process, and I stopped speaking, realizing I had said too much.

Poe rolled from the bed, crashed to the floor and grabbed a pair of trousers. "Villain!" He hurled this accusation as he hurriedly dressed. The little author ignored my entreaties, would not speak to me again. My attempts to placate him had no discernible effect. When I reached out to him, he recoiled violently from my touch.

Poe's disheveled silhouette ahead of the slamming door was the last I ever saw of him.

In his hurry to flee my company, he'd dressed himself in my clothes. Thinking he might realize his mistake, I waited for a time, but he did not return. Finally I rose and dressed, struggling into his smaller articles of clothing and mulling the morning's dramatic chain of events. I faced the looking-glass alone, with a curious lump of sorrow lodged in my throat.

Less than a week later, I found myself seated before the same bow window in the same coffee house along the same thoroughfare in Baltimore. Once again, the coffee grew cold. My cigar remained unlit and forgotten. But this time I ignored the endless throng of passersby on the street below. My attention was focused instead on a write-up in the latest newspaper. Apparently, the same morning he'd left my company, my author friend encountered one Joseph Walker, who believed him to be "in great distress, and in need of immediate assistance." Poe had been taken to the Washington College Hospital. Had I known his whereabouts, I would have tried to shed some light on the situation or assisted in some way. According to the article, he even called my name, though no one present knew who I was or how to contact me. And how could they? Our meeting came about by chance. Whether Poe desired my company or if he cursed my name for preying upon his sanity with revelations of my wickedness, I know not. I sat there reading and rereading the tragic news as hot tears burned my cheeks.

Thus my story comes to an end. I fear I am utterly lost. Life and death are equally cruel jests. I have shared one dark secret in the faintest hope of easing my conscience. But I say again, there are some secrets that should never be told. I made a colossal blunder once before and a troubled genius paid for it with his sanity and his life. Guilt over my depraved desires pushes me to the cusp of madness, but what those interests may be must remain a secret. The burden must be mine to bear alone.

THE DRACULA CLUB

Mitzi Szereto

What was a small-town Goth chick from the farmlands of Ohio, USA doing in Dracula Country? Maybe it was the result of watching too many of those old Hammer films on TV, yet something had been pulling me to that part of the world for as long as I can remember. Did it matter that Bran Castle is nothing but a tourist attraction and Poenari Castle may or may *not* be connected to vampire legend depending on whether you choose to believe that Vlad the Impaler was an actual vampire?

But I went on these pilgrimages anyway, joining up with a tour group that had an English-language guide, making the rounds in a rickety coach driven by a crazed Romanian with a fetish for taking treacherous mountain turns too quickly. The Carpathians are not for the faint of heart. The wildest it ever got in rural Ohio was when an Amish buggy pulled into an intersection and the horse suddenly decided to take a dump.

I knew early on that my calling to the Old Country was not the result of some youthful fancy, which was how my family, schoolmates and teachers had always dismissed it. There's not a huge amount of interest in Transylvania where I'm from, nor is there a huge amount of interest in Goth culture. Everyone thought I was crazy to be working all hours answering phones in a grubby warehouse office in the daytime (where no one had to look at me), then serving up greasy fast food and watery ice cream at the Dairy Queen in the evening (where I *could* be seen, but the country bumpkins and hot-rodding juvies were usually too drunk on cheap beer to care).

But I had a plan—and it was to save up enough money to fund my trip to Romania and have a bit left over to keep me going until I figured out how to earn a living. What did I care what the local yokels thought of me or my goals? I'd always been an outcast with my dyed black hair and my face and body piercings, my heavy black eye makeup and weird black clothes. The only people back home who dressed in black were the Amish—and they sure as hell weren't Goth.

I was endlessly taunted at school about being a vampire who slept in a coffin. "The President of the Dracula Club," was their nickname for me, among others too nasty to bear repeating. When a grave in the local cemetery had been disturbed, I was the one all fingers pointed to. Police officers had even gone to my house to question me. The fact that I'd been upstairs asleep in my bedroom all night with the door locked against my corn-fed Brady Bunch parents was of no interest to the residents of our shitty little town. (The cops eventually laid off, since they couldn't pin anything on me.) From that moment on I knew I had to get out of that burg as soon as I reached the age at which I would be legally allowed to leave the dominion of my parents. It was a relief to everyone when I finally did, including one of the boys I occasionally got it on with—a local meth dealer who claimed his association with me was weirding out his customers.

My parents never did understand how they'd managed to produce such a freak of a daughter. "Why can't you be more like that nice Katie McDonald?" they'd always ask, referring to the local minister's daughter who'd been in both junior and senior year with me—a Miss-Goody-Two-Shoes blonde who everyone thought was so pure and proper, despite the fact that she could usually be found giving blow jobs to the scuzzy jocks on our football team when she wasn't helping her old man at church. Sometimes she'd turn up in class with some guy's leftovers still on her chin, only to wipe it away when someone pointed it out to her, claiming she'd just been eating yogurt before the bell rang. And everyone actually bought this bullshit, since the minister's daughter would never tell a lie, right? Even my brothers and sisters sang her praises, since they too were ashamed of me, never wanting to admit my blood connection to them. As if everyone in town didn't already know....

Maybe I *should've* been more like Katie McDonald. At least then I'd have been popular and well liked by everyone, and my family might've been proud of me instead of hanging their heads as if I were the spawn of Charles Manson. The fact that I'd need to get my stomach pumped every week from all that football-team come I'd swallowed, well...I guess that would've been a happy trade-off for the folks.

I needed to get out of that stifling hell before it swallowed me up like it did everyone else.

So I went to Transylvania with my brand-new passport, with no intention of ever returning to the land that had issued it to me. Unlike the more popular European destinations that all the American kids went flocking to with their scruffy backpacks and their slave-like willingness to work illegally for below a wage anyone native would've accepted, I doubted if anyone from Romanian immigration would come looking for me in Transylvania when my tourist visa ran out. I could disappear off the radar—which suited me just fine. I figured I could stay there indefinitely, provided I kept myself going financially and picked up enough of the language to communicate with the locals. Romanian sounded like Italian to me—and I'd taken a couple of years of Italian in high school, which had also earned me points in the freak department, since nearly everyone interested in a foreign language took either Spanish or French; it was a miracle the Italian teacher managed to keep her job.

I might've been a small-town girl, but stupid I was not. Which is why I didn't fall for all the spooky shenanigans on those Transylvanian castle tours. Oh, they were entertaining and all, not to mention steeped in atmosphere. I had to do it; it was a rite of passage. But I wanted to find the *real* Dracula culture. I knew it existed somewhere in Transylvania. It was simply a matter of finding it.

I stayed in a small guesthouse on a back street in the medieval city of Sighisoara, the birthplace of the aforementioned Vlad the Impaler. The place was cheap and reasonably clean and within walking distance to taverns and shops and the Internet café. I should add that a lot of the shops sold that touristy Dracula crap. I thought of mailing some Dracula postcards back home to Ohio, but decided not to waste my rapidly dwindling finances. Instead I took the money I'd have blown on souvenirs for the family and went to the Bererie restaurant and tavern, which had once been Vlad's house and which had now become my local hangout. That so many people chose to eat and drink in a place that had once belonged to a man who got off on...um...*impaling* people is a bit bizarre, I admit. Yet so too is the fact that I experienced a sexual frisson from eating and drinking in the joint. I've always been a bit weird in my sexual tastes. I mean, any girl who masturbates to pictures of vampires in various blood-sucking poses has to be a bit touched in the head, right? I knew that Prince Vlad wasn't technically a vampire in the Count Dracula sense, but imagining him doing his worst prompted me to reach beneath the table (and my skirt) and enjoy a stealthy orgasm as the other patrons went about with their eating and drinking, chasing my pleasure with a hearty swig from a—you guessed it—Drax beer.

My little pleasures became increasingly intoxicating (along with all the beer I'd drink) as I wondered if anyone in the tavern was aware of my clandestine activities. Although I never caught anyone looking in my direction, that didn't take away the thrill of self-pleasure in a public place. I always claimed the same small table in a corner. It seemed as if it were reserved for me, since no one else ever sat there. I suppose it was possible someone might have been aware of what I was doing. I liked to imagine a handsome Gypsy boy watching me and maybe doing likewise, stroking his handsome Gypsy cock in time with the fluttering strokes of my fingers between my thighs.

There were plenty of Gypsy boys in the villages and towns and cities of Transylvania, and I admit I liked the idea of bedding a few, with their curly dark hair and dramatic features. They sure beat the hell out of those Wonder-Bread boys from the high-school football team. I'm sure I had an idealized image of these Gypsies and their lives as opposed to the grimmer reality, which often included working in organized gangs to beg or thieve off Western tourists, especially Americans with their loud blaring voices and lack of street smarts. Some of the guidebooks I'd read warned against falling prey to them and other *maradona,* but hey, I like to live dangerously.

One night two gorgeous boys approached my table, planting themselves on the two empty chairs and making themselves at home, their jet eyes daring me to protest. I didn't. We were all drinking the same touristy flavorless Drax beer (which has a bloodthirsty vampire on the label) and they waved to the barmaid to bring us three more. I was still breathless from the last quivers of my climax and could feel the flush on my cheeks. It's not the same as a flush of embarrassment or the flush of being in an overly warm room. There's no mistaking *this* kind of flush—and these two definitely didn't mistake it. They looked at me intently, their lips eventually breaking into broad smiles. I was pleased to note that their teeth were in better condition than those belonging to most of the local population and consisted of more enamel than gold. If it weren't for their features and stilted English, I might have mistaken the owners of those teeth for American.

"I am Dragos," said the one who looked slightly older, though not by much. "And this is Bela." He gestured with his dark head of curls toward his friend.

"Bela?" I repeated, trying not to laugh because he shared the same first name as Bela Lugosi, the Hungarian actor who'd played in the original Dracula films.

"You find it funny, yes?" he said, as if reading my mind.

"Not at all!" I didn't sound convincing even to myself.

Bela smiled, apparently forgiving the silly American tourist who'd grown up surrounded by names no more exotic than Seth, Jacob or Cory. "Dracula," he said, the expression in his eyes playful as he stared at my neck. His tongue licked over his lips, as if savoring the remnants of the blood sucked from his latest victim.

This time I had to laugh. "Yes! How did you know that's who I was thinking of?"

"Bela is a common name in this part of Europe, but not so common for foreigners, yes?" His lips stretched into a smile and I could feel it reaching down inside me. He hadn't physically touched me, but I felt very touched.

Dragos reached for my hand—the one I'd just been using to stimulate myself—and pressed it against his lips. I felt my face growing even hotter as I wondered if he could smell me on my fingers—a warmth which turned to fire when his tongue darted out to lick my fingertips. If he hadn't been able to smell me he could taste me—and judging from his expression, he liked it. I wasn't sure whether to be mortified or aroused. Some prim moral conviction told me to slap his face. But I didn't want to.

I tried to regain my composure by indicating my interest in the pack of cigarettes I saw sticking out of his shirt pocket. He offered me one, lighting it in an Old World courtly way, the complete opposite of the fumbling Ohio country boys. They were unfiltered. I spent a couple of minutes taking long drags on it, burning it down to a stub in record time and enjoying that raw burn in my throat that you just can't get with filtered cigarettes. I felt a need to fill the silence, since neither of them seemed inclined to say anything further. "So are you two Gypsies?" I asked, not caring how stupid the question sounded. It felt as if I could have said anything, regardless of how rude or ridiculous and it wouldn't have mattered to them.

"We are Gypsies if you desire us to be," replied Dragos with a smile. "We are *anything* you desire us to be."

Desire. What an odd choice of word to use. But then, he

was probably translating his thoughts from Romanian into English as he went along; maybe he wasn't aware of the erotic connotation the word evoked. On the other hand, maybe he was. His pronouncement sent a postorgasmic flutter through me. I'd never met boys like this. I was in way over my head, and I didn't care.

"You are tourist to Transylvania?" asked Bela.

"Well, yes and no."

I could see my statement confused them so I tried to clarify it, feeling a need to defend myself. "Actually, I've come here to live." Until now it had felt like a childish fantasy, but saying it out loud suddenly made it real. Yes, I *had* come here to live. I smiled, pleased with myself, despite the fact that I had a long way to go before I'd be settled and self-sustaining in my new country.

"Ahh, but that is splendid!" cried Dragos. "You will find much joy here. I am certain of it."

I believed him. Don't ask me why, but I believed him. Had I only known then what manner of joy it was that I would eventually find....

From that point on Dragos, Bela and I met every evening to consume vast quantities of beer, supplementing it with regional dishes such as *sarmale* (essentially stuffed cabbage) and *ciorba de burta* (tripe soup). They paid. I didn't complain. My funds were limited and I knew I would need to start looking for work soon. I'd considered getting a job in one of the local taverns serving food and drink (if I were lucky) or else cleaning (if I were not so lucky). It seemed like the easiest way forward and one that wouldn't require too much of me when it came to providing immigration paperwork, though I doubted anyone in these Transylvanian mountains gave a flying fuck about such formalities.

Eventually we stopped going to the Bererie. Instead Dragos and Bela drove me in their old Communist-issue banger to the small villages deep in the Carpathians to experience "the *real* Transylvania." Here the taverns were darker and smokier and frequented by people with suspicious eyes and an inability to smile. This was Old Transylvania, filled with peasants and Gypsies and others for whom the brutal iron fist of Ceaușescu's rule hadn't yet faded. There were no Dracula postcards sold in these villages. Nor was there any touristy Drax beer sold in the taverns or shops. Instead we switched to Ursus black beer—a dark lager with character, drinking as if we wouldn't live to see another day, eating rustic bread accompanied by *bulz ciobanesc*, the tasty cheese dumplings they made in this part of the world.

I had no fear of being driven at night by Dragos and Bela to these isolated villages. In the same circumstances in America my nude and raped body would have already been found along the roadside being pecked over by vultures, but for some reason I felt completely safe with these two young men who never said much about themselves or where they were from. Something was happening between us, and by *us* I don't mean Dragos with me or me with Bela—I mean me with *both* Dragos and Bela. They took turns driving out into the countryside while I sat on the lap of whoever occupied the passenger seat, my black skirt hitched up to my waist and my black panties discarded on the floor of the car, my thighs brazenly wide as fingers teased and explored me until I'd puddled a climax onto the trousers of whichever boy was beneath me. Whoever drove would lean in for a kiss and fondle my breasts, which had been bared from my top, the nipples hard as iron pellets from the cold mountain air blowing in through the open windows, which were stuck fast and could not be rolled shut. The heater in the car didn't work either, but I didn't notice the chill. My body was burning up with a lust it had never experienced back in Ohio. Had snow been blowing onto my bare sex I wouldn't have noticed.

Dragos and Bela never asked for permission; they just *did*. I had no objections. I was becoming someone else, transforming into a being that was fearful of nothing. I felt as if I'd always belonged in this staggeringly beautiful and dramatic landscape that had given birth to so much legend and bloodshed. Something told me I would never leave.

By our third trip into the mountains, I was impaling myself upon the erect flesh beneath me, riding it as we bumped along the rutted roads into the thick blackness of the Transylvanian night, only to repeat the process on the way back with the boy who'd been driving earlier, my sex still slick and widened from his friend. We didn't use condoms. Dragos and Bela weren't worried about catching anything, so I wasn't worried either. No one even mentioned them. Condoms belonged to some other world—a world full of disease and noise and hypocrisy. We were invincible and nothing could divert us from this road of lust we were traveling. Sometimes we pulled over to the side of the road, clambering into the torn backseat with its stuffing spilling out like guts so that they could both have me at once. One would be on top of and inside me, my feet planted wide on the ceiling of the car, while the other was crammed into the small space on the floor, his flesh filling my mouth. I'd then swivel around on the seat, switching who occupied which orifice until I'd become a human metronome in a sexual game of musical chairs.

Through the open windows I could hear the howling and

baying of wolves, bringing to mind that line spoken by Count Dracula about children of the night and what beautiful music they make. The sound *was* beautiful and I'd come with a violent shudder, its melody singing in my ears, the harsher music of Dragos and Bela as they filled me with their Gypsy seed accompanying it. Ohio was a very long way away by then. I no longer bothered with Internet cafés and messages home. I had vanished into the Transylvanian ether.

One evening while we sat eating and drinking at our favorite tavern, Dragos informed me that they would be taking me home. I was curious about where they lived and how they lived, since I knew nothing about them. From the moment we'd met nearly every question I put forth to them was met with the response of "If you desire us to be"—yet I knew all I needed to know and didn't feel the need to press them for details. I figured if they wanted or needed for me to know something, they would tell me.

The cemetery was unexpected.

Most of the headstones had their engravings worn off, and those that were still legible displayed dates going back centuries. On first glance these modest places of rest appeared to belong to peasants from the neighboring village, but as Dragos and Bela led me deeper into the misty murk hanging low over the earth with nothing to aid us but an oil lantern and what light there was from the half-moon above, I discovered there was more here than I'd believed. An old crypt held court at the farthermost part of the cemetery, declaring itself on a higher social stratum than that of its humble neighbors. Dragos and Bela each took my hand and led me inside.

A lone stone coffin sat elevated on a pedestal. The occupant didn't have any family or loved ones to share the space with or else he or she hadn't been too popular, since it was the only coffin here. Dragos explained in his stilted English that it had at one time contained the remains of a wealthy landowner. I assumed that whatever was left of this landowner had been relocated elsewhere, perhaps to somewhat grander surroundings such as a family cemetery on a castle estate, but Dragos soon put that notion to rest when he admitted that he and Bela had been the ones responsible for the disinterring.

It appeared that my two Transylvanian lovers were in the habit of digging up dead bodies.

The fact that I was in the middle of a dark and remote cemetery somewhere in the Carpathian Mountains with two strong young males who had no qualms about removing the remains of the dead from their coffins should have sent me screaming into the night. It didn't. If anything, it turned me on, and I had to keep my hand from reaching beneath my skirt to get off, since I still had a small amount of propriety left.

"This is where we sleep," said Bela as he set the lantern down on a stone ledge. It cast the interior of the crypt in a soft yellow glow that made it rather cozy despite the smell of decay and the rat droppings.

"Excuse me?" I asked, not certain I'd heard him correctly. Surely he didn't mean *inside* the stone coffin?

Dragos laughed and reached out to touch my cheek, his fingers cascading downward like rippling waves over the front of my black silk vest top, stopping to undo the laces and expose my breasts. Bela's hands reached from behind to ease the garment off my shoulders and arms until I was naked from the waist up. It was cold and dank inside the crypt and the flesh of my nipples puckered. Dragos took one into his mouth, drawing hard upon it until it hurt, then moving on to its twin. I felt Bela pressing against me, the rigidness in his jeans working to find a home within the crease of my backside, which was protected only by the gauzy black fabric of my skirt. I was so wet by then that my thighs felt glued together. My panties were probably still on the floor of the car. Then I remembered that Dragos had thrown them out of the car window, saying that I wouldn't be needing them anymore. I began to wonder if the same fate might befall my skirt and top and maybe even my expensive black buckle-up boots I'd ordered online from a Goth clothing shop in England. They'd cost me three weeks' salary from both my jobs combined. Maybe Dragos and Bela planned to keep me here as their cemetery slave, naked and unable to refuse their desires.

I liked the idea.

Dragos removed his hand from the vicinity of my breasts to undo the silver skull buckle on my belt, followed by the buttons that fastened my skirt at the waist. The gauzy silk slithered to the floor in a black puddle that looked like blood in the lamp-light. I stood there in the chilly crypt in nothing but my boots until Dragos decided to turn his attention to those as well, and then I was left wearing only my black thigh-high Lycra socks. Dropping into a crouch, he grasped my hips and pulled my pelvis toward him, consuming me with a tongue so hot it felt as if it would scorch my flesh, his nails digging into the cheeks of my buttocks, breaking through the skin like tiny blades. When Bela dropped down behind me and used his tongue to do the same with an orifice that no boy had ever touched, not even to tease with a fingertip, I felt my knees giving way. My pleasure rose up and erupted from me in a sound that couldn't possibly have come from a human mouth, and yet it had.

Standing up, Dragos turned his attention to the coffin. He

wedged his palms beneath the lid, hoisting it open as if the stone weighed no more than cardboard. I could see in the light that it was empty. The interior looked surprisingly clean and was upholstered in a cushioned red silk that was the shade of freshly spilled blood. The fabric had been attached via a series of small fasteners drilled into the stone. I suspected the swanky decor had to be Dragos and Bela's handiwork, since any original fabric would have worn down to dust by now, as would the occupant had he still been residing there.

Suddenly the air in the crypt didn't feel quite so cold as it had earlier, though that might have been a result of the heat of our aroused bodies rather than anything supernatural in our surroundings. I had no idea when he'd done it, but Dragos had unzipped his fly and his cock was thrusting out from his jeans, pointing high with youthful eagerness. This time it was I who fell to my knees.

He tasted good, like a mixture of old wine and sage honey, as he pushed into my mouth, coming quickly and without a lot of fanfare. I liked boys who didn't do the whole grunting and groaning thing. I found it distracting and crude; it always made me want to burst out laughing, as did their distorted expressions when they came. Dragos's face remained dignified and beautiful as he emptied his pleasure down my throat, making me more conscious of my own expression and how I must have looked to him with his hard flesh stuffed into my mouth. I pivoted around to do the same to Bela, who tasted mostly of me, since he'd been inside me on the drive over. He also came quickly and I swallowed it just as I had with Dragos, experiencing no sense of revulsion like I always did with boys back home. I wanted to stay with them inside that little crypt forever.

Dragos took my hand and assisted me up from the floor,

kissing it in his usual courtly way. "You will join us in our bed please?" he asked formally, indicating the coffin, its upraised lid seeming to invite us inside.

How could I refuse?

Stripping off their clothing and shoes, they left everything in a heap on the floor and we three climbed into the coffin. After a clever arrangement of our bodies that consisted of Bela lying beneath me, Dragos lying on top of me facing down and me lying between them facing up, Dragos stretched an arm behind him to lower the lid until the last sliver of light had gone, leaving us in absolute blackness. Not so much as a thread's width of light crept through the edges of the coffin lid. I wondered if we might suffocate, yet I felt neither afraid nor worried. I knew that I was where I was meant to be.

Dragos and Bela took control of my body, kissing, stroking, probing. At times I could feel the presence of the wealthy land-owner whom they had displaced. I was certain there were more than two pairs of hands on my body and more than two sighing voices in my ears. I could even feel an icy tongue licking the same places that Dragos and Bela had licked earlier—licking with a frantic and tragic desperation neither of them had ever likely experienced. Had I lost my mind from being shut inside a centuries-old stone coffin with young men whose surnames I didn't even know? Maybe.

Or maybe not.

When I felt myself being penetrated front and back, the sensation of being stretched, then split in half truly did tease me with insanity—the insanity reaching fruition when something hard and cylindrical and as icy cold as death began to force its way into my mouth. I knew immediately what it was—and it didn't belong to Dragos or Bela, whose own versions were occupied elsewhere. I tasted dried flowers and vinegar and I closed my lips around it in acceptance, feeling it begin to warm against my tongue. My insanity continued long into the night, our bodies crushing and grinding together...until the air in the coffin was no more, and we became one with the dead.

Moonfall

Rose de Fer

T he frozen night was filled with menace. An owl hooted, its call eerie and desolate. Icicles hung from the skeletal trees like the bared fangs and talons of some fantastical creature. All at once the silence was shattered by the thundering of horses' hooves on the cold ground as a carriage hurtled along the road. Overhanging branches clutched at the vehicle as it made its way through the forest, but nothing could impede its passage. The driver whipped the horses and they galloped on, drawing ever nearer to their destination.

Black spires clawed at the sky as an imposing façade hove into view. The carriage rounded a turn and headed up a long and winding drive toward the dark stone manor house where a guard was waiting to unlock the heavy iron gate. Like the arms of a metal giant, the gate swung open, shrieking on its rusty hinges. A pale face peered out from within the carriage as it drove past the carved plaque on the gatepost: THORNCROFT ASYLUM FOR THE INCURABLY INSANE.

When they reached the front door the driver reined the

horses in. They stamped and snorted like captured dragons, their breath steaming. A tall gentleman stood in the shadows of the arched doorway. He gave a single nod and the coachman opened the door of the carriage. Two other men hastened to assist the occupant out.

The young woman blinked in confusion, feeling as though she had just woken from a strange dream. She had only a vague memory of the journey, and it took her a moment to register where she was. She struggled at first, but the men were strong and she knew she had no hope of resisting their firm grip.

"Come along, miss," one of them said, not unkindly. "You'll be quite safe inside."

Madeleine Chancery allowed herself to be lifted from the carriage and she puzzled at the strange sensation as her bare feet touched the snowy ground. Where were her shoes? A glance down at herself showed that her dress was in tatters. She caught her reflection in the gleaming shell of the carriage and gave a startled little cry. She looked a fright. Her hair fell in wild blonde tangles about her face, which was smeared with mud.

"Mrs. Chancery."

The tall man descended the steps and Madeleine peered up at him. She knew him, of course. Dr. Charles Thorncroft. James's brother. Panic leapt in her chest. Had he seen them together? Did he know of their trysts? Worse: had he told her husband?

But instead of accusing her, he extended his hand as though she were alighting at the home of someone hosting a midnight ball. "Welcome, my dear," he said. "You will be very comfortable here. Of that I can assure you."

Dazed, she offered her own hand without thinking and he

took it, frowning slightly at the sight. It wasn't just dirty; it was streaked with what looked like dried blood.

She gasped and yanked it back, wrapping her arms around herself. "Why am I here?" she asked at last.

"We'll talk inside," said Dr. Thorncroft pleasantly, his deep voice booming in the stillness. "A warm fire. Perhaps a little brandy to take away the chill and calm your nerves?"

Madeleine glanced warily at the men on either side of her. Running away would be utterly pointless and only serve to humiliate her further. She could never hope to escape and even if she did, she would surely freeze to death.

"Very well," she said, lifting her head proudly and trying to retain some dignity. "You can explain to me why Henry had me abducted in the night and brought to this—this place."

She followed Dr. Thorncroft inside, taking in her surroundings with wide eyes. Her feet tingled against the mosaic tiles of the elegant entryway as he led her down a long corridor. Gaslight flickered along the oak-paneled walls, and from somewhere deep within the building came a scream. She froze, gazing with horror up into the darkness of the curved staircase.

She had a very bad feeling about this place. And most especially this man.

"Nothing for you to concern yourself with," Dr. Thorncroft said darkly. "Not everyone here is as compliant as I know you will be."

He met her eyes for a long, uncomfortable moment before taking her arm and guiding her firmly away.

Madeleine was startled at her body's strange response to him as she allowed herself to be led to the room at the end of the corridor. He was as strikingly handsome as his brother and there was something in his authoritative tone that made her body tingle in spite of her apprehension.

Shadows leapt along the walls of the room he led her to, thrown by the blazing fire in the hearth. She sank to her knees before it and stretched out her hands, more for the opportunity to turn away from her host than for warmth. She sensed the doctor standing behind her, watching. Heat flooded her face. She felt horribly exposed in her tattered clothes and bare feet. But, strangely, the feeling of vulnerability wasn't entirely disagreeable. She had no idea how she had come to be in such a state but her adventure must have been a pleasant one. Her sex pulsed, hot and wet, both with recent satisfaction and a craving for more. Had she been with James? She was distressed to find she couldn't remember.

After a moment she heard the clink of glass and she readied herself to face him again. She mustn't let him see her fear or confusion. She must be calm. There was a rational explanation for all this and once they got to the bottom of it she could send for her things, dress herself and leave.

"Here you are," he said.

He held out a glass of brandy, which she drank at once, grateful for the pleasant burn of the liquid and the courage she knew the alcohol would lend her. It was nice brandy, if surprisingly potent. Almost at once she felt a little dizzy, no doubt an effect of her nervousness. She swallowed the rest of the brandy and arranged her features into a smile. Then she turned to look up at Dr. Thorncroft.

"It's most kind of you," she said in as simpering a voice as she could muster. "Now suppose you tell me what this is all about, and then I can be on my way."

Thorncroft returned her smile but there was no warmth in

it. "Mrs. Chancery," he said, measuring his words as though relishing their delivery, "you won't be going anywhere."

She looked down at her empty glass as her vision began to blur. Then all was darkness.

James Thorncroft was horrified to learn that Madeleine had been committed to his brother's asylum. He had never seen her exhibit any sign of mental illness. In fact, their stolen moments together were proof that she was a woman who knew her own mind very well and was in full possession of her faculties.

He pictured her slate-gray eyes, her sensual lips and flaxen hair, the tantalizing glimpse of creamy bosom allowed by her décolletage. But her charms did not end there; she was as clever as she was beautiful. And he had loved her since the day he'd first laid eyes on her, the day her husband had brought her to the zoo to see the animals James kept.

They had locked gazes in the aviary, light-headed with desire. The shrieking of jungle birds faded to a pleasant hum in the background as they stared at each other like two wild creatures recognizing their perfect mate. Madeleine had slipped away that evening to see him, then again on subsequent evenings. Henry was oblivious, interested more in cards and horses than his beautiful, neglected wife. Still, the lovers had been careful. They had never been seen together except under the most innocent of circumstances. Had Henry nonetheless discovered the truth and had his wife locked up by way of revenge? The thought made James shudder.

Dr. Thorncroft interrupted his thoughts.

"A most intriguing case," he said, his eyes glittering. "She's a prize specimen. Quite the jewel in my collection."

"But surely this is no place for a lady," James protested.

"Oh, she is no delicate maiden held captive in a tower. The woman suffers from a very rare disorder. I've never come across another case like it before. It's a condition I have chosen to call Somnambulophrenia. I've already begun writing a paper on it for the Royal College." Thorncroft steepled his fingers and smiled as though basking in the glory.

James frowned, puzzling over the name. "She sleepwalks? That warrants locking her up in here?"

Thorncroft gave an exasperated sigh. "My dear brother, it is hardly a case of mere sleepwalking. It's not even apparent whether she is actually asleep at all. She wanders under the influence of her own disordered mind."

"Do you mean she's pretending?"

"Not quite. I'm sure she believes she sleepwalks. Her periods of amnesia seem genuine enough. That suggests that whatever mischief takes place during these episodes is too traumatic to recall. And this delusion means she is a danger not only to herself but to anyone with whom she comes into contact in her wandering state. According to her husband, she has returned home many a night in a most unladylike condition, her clothes torn, her hair in disarray. Naturally, he feared for her safety, as do I."

"Naturally," James said with a contemptuous snort. He knew full well why Madeleine occasionally returned home in a state of disarray and it had nothing to do with sleepwalking. "One can hardly take his word for it. I happen to know Mr. Henry Chancery and I can assure you that he is no gentleman. I suspect his account is greatly exaggerated. And to what purpose? Why, it's common knowledge that he was nearly penniless when he met and courted Madeleine Wingate."

Thorncroft laughed. "Are you implying that he married her

for her fortune? Honestly, I never thought you were the type to indulge in ladies' gossip."

James bristled, but kept his voice even. "I'm telling you that not only did he marry her for her fortune, he had her committed so as to gain control of it. How much did he pay you to have her certified insane? I expect your fee was not inconsiderable."

His words had clearly struck a nerve. Thorncroft's eyes narrowed and his jaw worked for a few seconds before he spoke again. "I find your insinuation highly offensive." Then he sat back in his chair, regarding James with a challenging smile. "For your information, this lady could hold the key to the entire future of medical science."

James waited for him to elaborate but it was obvious he wanted to be asked. "Very well. What is this great discovery you're clearly very keen to tell me about?"

Thorncroft tapped a thick sheaf of papers stacked to one side of his desk. "She has the most extraordinary healing properties."

Whatever he'd been expecting, this took him by surprise. "What do you mean?"

"I mean that she heals as if by magic. A small cut might vanish in a matter of minutes while a more serious injury can last several days. But the healing process is always the same: rapid and absolute. She has no scars, not a single blemish. And you can be assured that I have examined her very thoroughly."

James didn't like the gleam in his brother's eyes, didn't like to wonder just how he had come by this peculiar discovery.

"I can see you don't approve," Thorncroft said. "If it sets your mind at ease, let me reassure you that the lady feels no pain."

"Just because you inject her with drugs—"

"No, no, no! I mean she doesn't feel pain. Doesn't experience it. At all. It's as though her pain receptors are nonexistent. And yet she clearly feels pleasure and stimulation. Rather too much, in fact. Whatever strange processes are at work in her, there is certainly an element of sexual hysteria. She is capable of the most unseemly and wanton behavior."

That much was true at least. It was one of the things he loved about her. Madeleine was no repressed gentlewoman; she was a sensualist, like him.

"I dare say," Thorncroft continued, "she even takes some perverse pleasure in our little sessions. Clearly there is no place for her in polite society. It's best that she remain here, where she can be looked after. So you needn't worry about her. She's in safe hands."

James couldn't believe what he was hearing. The poor woman suffered from nothing more than a healthy sexual appetite and a high pain threshold. But because she also had a fondness for moonlight strolls, she was locked up like a common lunatic while her greedy husband squandered her fortune.

"So what you're telling me is that she's become some sort of laboratory specimen, a creature to be experimented on for the rest of her days."

Thorncroft waved a hand dismissively. "I should have known you were too sensitive to appreciate my work. It involves rather more than traipsing about the globe catching butterflies and observing new species of bird. Now, if you don't mind, I have much to do. I suggest you run along back to your little pets and leave the medical science to me."

James drew back from his brother's cold words and patronizing tone. "I'm sorry you think so little of my own field of study," he said, rising to leave. "It is perhaps fair to say that

I know more about animals than people, but I cannot abide cruelty to either species. In any case, it's a small consolation to me to see that at least one of us inherited our parents' sense of compassion. I'll show myself out."

With that he turned on his heel and left, closing the door to his brother's study with some force. As the housekeeper fetched his overcoat and walking stick he peered up the stairs. Madeleine was up there somewhere, imprisoned against her will and subjected to appalling treatment. Now that he knew the full extent of his brother's unsavory methods he had no intention of leaving his beloved at the mercy of them.

It had been more than three weeks since Madeleine had found herself an inmate of the asylum. At first she had rebelled, but when her haughty demeanor got her nowhere she tried other tacks—charm, bribery, even violence. Nothing worked.

The orderlies were kind and she'd done her best to exploit that kindness, begging them to let her out, implying that it was their employer who was mad and not she. But that was a ploy they had clearly seen before, from lesser personages than her.

Her first week had been a very unhappy one. How she had cursed Henry for engineering her imprisonment, for humiliating her and for putting her at the mercy of a man like Dr. Thorncroft. But however loath she was to admit it, there was, after all, something not right with her. That night hadn't been the first time she'd woken to find herself muddy and disheveled, with no memory of events.

Dr. Thorncroft had noticed right away how her superficial cuts and abrasions vanished as if by magic. And Madeleine had been just as fascinated. As a test one night she'd scraped her arm along one of the iron bars of her window. Blood welled along the cut in a bright vivid line before trickling over her arm and dripping onto the floor. Not a serious injury, but a painful one. Or rather—one that should have been painful. She felt the skin separate, felt the blood rising to the surface before spilling out, but curiously, it hadn't hurt. On the contrary, she had felt stimulated by it. Aroused.

Dr. Thorncroft had since come to call her strange response "hysteria," insisting that sexual excitement was unnatural in women. How unlike his brother he was! James didn't find her passion in the least disturbing. On the contrary, he celebrated it.

The doctor often spoke of Madeleine as though she were merely an experimental subject and not a patient and she wondered whether his clinical detachment might be his undoing. If he focused exclusively on her physical responses, he would be blind to any plotting and scheming. He would certainly never imagine her capable of getting the better of him. And she gave him plenty to focus on by way of distraction.

After watching her self-inflicted cut stitch itself up within minutes, leaving no trace of a scar, Madeleine had decided to let the doctor do as he wished with her. He could perform his tests and she would gaze at him, wide-eyed and hopeful that he could cure the ludicrous condition he had invented for her. It was abnormal, he claimed, for a woman to wander as she did, with no memory of her actions or how she came to be in such a state afterward. He was certain that her remarkable healing abilities were related to the condition somehow; he just couldn't find the link.

But Madeleine had her suspicions.

She was coming to understand much about herself and her body's strange responses and abilities. And as she watched the moon each night through her window she felt more and more drawn to its ghostly blue light. She felt its pull, sensed its exertions on the tides within her body. As the moon waxed, so had her initial fury at being brought here. It shrank to a sliver in the sky, a sharp and gleaming thorn. Or perhaps it was a claw. Something to rend and tear. Something animal and alive. Night after night she watched it swell, opening like an eye fixed just on her.

And with the swelling of the moon came a swelling of desire. She was unashamed of her "perverse" feelings; resisting them was what felt truly unnatural.

For as long as she could remember, her mind had reeled with fantasies. Highwaymen who waylaid her and spirited her away, pinning her down in the wild forest and taking it in turns to ravish her. Oriental traders who captured her and herded her onto an auction block with other ladies, there to be sold to the highest bidder. She had read of such encounters in books. Lurid novels Henry disapproved of. She read them in the privacy of her own room and it had been one such night that she'd first gone for a walk in the woods bordering the estate.

It was also the first night she had returned home disheveled, her hair tangled with leaves and twigs and her bare arms and legs streaked with blood. She was frightened by her misadventure and her lack of memory, but she refused to let Henry call a doctor. Once she'd considered telling James about it, but in the end decided to keep silent. It would have sounded mad. Ah, such bitter irony.

Now she was here, Henry having spied an advantage in her strange nightly escapades. And Dr. Thorncroft had spied a similar advantage, locking her up and studying her, no doubt for his own unscrupulous gain. If only she'd run off with James when he first suggested it!

No matter. It wouldn't be long before she was free. In the meantime she was using the doctor as much as he was using her, learning the limits of her body. Alas, his part in the adventure would not have a happy ending. The moon was getting bigger. Soon it would be full again. And he would have the answers he sought so eagerly.

Their last session had taken an unexpected turn. She was at the mercy of whatever strange effect the moon had on her and she had seduced him, fucking him like the sexual hysteric he believed her to be. She pressed her legs together, remembering.

As she slipped her hand up under her nightdress she closed her eyes. Her thoughts strayed first to James and then back to Dr. Thorncroft. She smiled as she imagined herself at the mercy of both men. They could pass her back and forth and have their wicked way with her.

As her fingers caressed the swollen nub of her clitoris she saw herself subjected to various exquisite indignities. James held her down while Dr. Thorncroft splayed her legs wide apart to peer closely at her, as though he might find the source of her affliction with his dexterous fingers. When she did not cooperate fully he punished her, using a riding whip across her back, her bottom, her breasts. Then James gathered her in his arms and kissed her better, his lips traveling down her throat to her breasts.

Her nipples tautened at the imagined pleasure and pain while wanton desire surged through her body. It did not take long before she was racked by spasms of ecstasy.

Outside the moon watched, waiting.

* * *

Thorncroft finished writing down his latest set of findings and got up to stretch. He was stiff and sore from the evening's exertions. Madeleine's hunger for physical sensation seemed to know no bounds. He had finally succumbed to her charms and was rather exhausted from the episode. Naturally, he wouldn't record that in his journal, but he had wanted to make notes on a few unusual observations.

Now he stood at the window, gazing out at the full moon and rubbing at the tense muscles in his arms. Her strength had been surprising, and it had taken all his effort to hold her down. She wanted it rough, she said, wanted to resist and be conquered, wanted him to hurt her.

"You can do anything to me," she panted, "anything at all and I'll heal."

And when he hesitated, she scratched him. He'd had to pin her down for his own safety, bruising her slender wrists. He was hardly surprised to find that the force excited her. She fought more, urging him on until he'd had no choice but to oblige, fucking her as he might a whore. She'd screamed her unnatural passion to the heavens until he gagged her, silencing her cries. And then, to his astonishment, she'd climaxed. He hadn't imagined that women were capable of it themselves. He knew of paroxysm in women only as a clinical treatment for hysteria. But then, Madeleine was no ordinary woman.

He'd left her then so he could return to his study. As he'd closed and locked her door behind him, he'd been unnerved by her low sultry laugh. There was something animal in it, something like a growl. But he'd shrugged away his uneasiness. The woman was mad, that was all.

As he turned back to his desk he heard a bloodcurdling

scream. Such sounds were common in the asylum, but this one chilled him to the bone. It was more animal than human and it went on for several seconds, tapering at last into a forlorn howl that was like some kind of hellish music. No woman could have produced such a sound.

And indeed, no woman had. There came another unearthly howl and this one was louder. Closer. He heard chaos throughout the building: shouts, running feet, breaking glass, splintering wood, a gunshot. An eerie silence followed, but it did not last long.

Something crashed through the window, landing in a shower of glass and lifting its white muzzle to reveal gleaming fangs. But it was the eyes that made him gasp with horror. The familiar slate-gray eyes were wild with a different kind of lust as the wolf knocked him easily to the floor and stood over him, growling.

He only had time to whisper her name before she tore his throat out.

When James arrived at the asylum he shuddered at the signs of chaos and carnage. Windows were broken, doors were torn off hinges, and what remained of his brother had been carried away by the police beneath a blood-soaked sheet. He felt only a small pang of sorrow. One couldn't provoke a wild animal with impunity. It was simply the law of nature, and Charles should have had more respect for it.

"The beast's upstairs," said the inspector. "We trapped it in a room for you."

James was relieved beyond measure to learn that they hadn't killed the wolf. When the strange spate of killings had first been reported in the papers months ago he had begged the police to let him take control of the animal should it ever be caught. Such a creature needed studying, he'd told them. It might be the only one of its kind. But it was only tonight, when the moon had risen high and full and he'd planned to rescue Madeleine, that he had made the vital, extraordinary connection.

"Thank you," he said, and made his way up the stairs. He could hear the wolf tearing the room apart as he approached.

The frightened constable guarding the door stared at him, wide-eyed. "You don't want to go in there, sir."

"It's all right," James said, holding out the jar of ether he had brought. "All you have to do is open it a crack."

The young man looked dubious, but did as he was told. James only had time to glimpse a white blur as he threw the bottle inside. The glass smashed on the hard wooden floor and the policeman slammed the door shut just in time. Then they listened while the wolf snarled and scrabbled at the door, desperate to escape the soporific fumes of the ether. After a while, all was quiet.

"Looks so peaceful when it's asleep," the constable said, keeping his distance.

"She," James said softly. He stroked the sleek fur as though the sleeping wolf were a beloved pet. Then he gathered her in his arms and carried her downstairs, where he locked her in the cage he'd brought with him. None of the policemen or orderlies dared to get close, so he was left to load his precious cargo into the carriage himself.

As the horses drew them away from the asylum he smiled down at the caged animal at his feet, gently stroking her face through the bars. "We're going home," he said.

* * *

When Madeleine woke she smelled straw, and she gradually became aware of the striped shadows on the floor. She felt groggy and slightly dizzy, as she always did after a night of—what had the doctor called it? Somnambulophrenia? Only this time something was different. With a start she realized what must have happened. She'd escaped the asylum and been arrested. She was in jail! Not only that: she was also stark naked.

She sat up in her straw-lined cell and stared around her in bewilderment. Naturally, she had never seen the inside of any jail, but she didn't imagine it should look like the drawing room of a house beyond the cell door. It was only when she tried to stand up that she understood. She wasn't in jail at all, but a cage.

"Good morning."

The voice startled her and for a moment she couldn't place it. Of all the voices she had heard in the past few weeks, James Thorncroft's was the one she had most longed to hear. She could hardly believe it was real.

"James?" Her own voice trembled as she said his name. "Is it really you?"

And then his smiling face was before her and she flushed deeply at his nearness, her body responding with hot little throbs. She could smell him, taste him. Her skin remembered his touch and wanted more. And her body held other strange memories. She had a sensation of having been stroked in the night while she slept. Of being carried. Of being watched over.

He unlocked the cage door and she crept out, feeling self-conscious and disoriented as she got shakily to her feet. "What happened?"

"You transformed," he said with a smile. "That's why you

can't remember anything. I hope you'll forgive me for locking you up, but it was the only way to keep us both safe. Here, put this on." He held out a dressing gown of rich blue velvet and she wrapped herself in it gratefully.

Her mind was still reeling from his casual explanation. "Transformed?"

"You become something else when the moon is full, Madeleine. A beautiful, exquisite creature who retains no memory of her human form. That's why you can't remember your 'sleepwalking.' That's why you heal so rapidly. And that's why you were imprisoned in that dreadful place. I think a part of me has known all along. I'm only sorry I didn't realize it sooner."

Madeleine thought back to the asylum and its terrible indignities, its delicious stimulations. Her body recalled the experiments, the pain that wasn't pain but something else, the cold clinical touch she'd found unbearably erotic. She blushed as she relived these moments in her mind and she pressed her legs together as a particular image came back to her. Dr. Thorncroft. He was pinning her down on the bed, plunging himself into her, exciting her beyond measure as he fucked her roughly, brutally, driven to his own special madness by her strange allure. It had been no dream.

But afterward, what had she done? In her mind were flashes of bright red, of screams and breaking glass. The heady taste of blood. She looked down at the floor.

"I fear I've done terrible things," she whispered.

But James lifted her head and made her look at him. "If you're feeling guilty about anything," he said firmly, "don't. When you're a wolf you respond to your natural instincts as any wolf would. And when you're human..." Fascination danced in his eyes. "Well, you're never quite human, are you? I don't think human rules apply to you at all. In any case, whatever you've done, it's in the past."

"So what's to become of me?" she said, her eyes filling with tears.

"Shhh. You're with me now, Madeleine. And I understand both aspects of you. I love both of you. The woman and the wolf."

Her gaze softened as she looked up at him. Yes, she could see in his eyes that he did. James knew and forgave every wicked thing she had done. Dr. Thorncroft had been right about her being dangerous; he'd simply been too arrogant to consider that she might be a threat to him. But she was safe with James. He would keep her secret and teach her about her other nature.

Heat pulsed between her thighs and she glanced down at the cage. "Are you going to...tame me?"

James's eyes gleamed with excitement to match her own. "If that's what you want." He stroked her face and she closed her eyes with a blissful sigh.

"You're what I want," she murmured. She opened the robe and slipped it off her shoulders. It pooled at her feet and she stood before him, brazenly naked.

His eyes roamed over her body, studying every soft, silky inch of her. Madeleine felt his gaze as though he were caressing her physically. She'd become used to being examined, inspected, scrutinized. But this time the exploration was not scientific. These were the eyes of a lover. Her lover. The man she was meant to be with.

James's hands followed where his eyes had gone, making her skin tingle with their warm softness. He drew his fingers down the line of her throat, along the curve of her ribs and back up between her breasts. Her nipples stiffened with the nearness of his touch as he circled them teasingly, allowing her to savor the anticipation. Then he took a step back and she watched hungrily as he removed his shirt and trousers.

Madeleine's heart pounded in rhythm with the throbbing between her legs. Her breathing grew shallow as she pressed herself against James's broad chest, basking in his warm, musky scent as she felt the hardness of his cock between them. Now that she understood her strange nature she knew why her senses were so acute. Everything—smells, taste and most of all touch—was a sweet torment of heightened stimulation. And it was with a wolf's primal lust that she climbed into his arms, wrapping her legs around his body.

He cupped her bottom with his hands as he carried her to the bed and laid her down. She writhed in the softness of the bedclothes, her sex a warm wet heat desperate for his touch. "Take me," she murmured. "I want to feel everything."

With a smile James lowered his mouth to hers, bruising her lips with his passion. Her tongue sought his, tangling sweetly as they kissed. Then she felt his knee between her legs, nudging them apart. Obediently, she arched her back, presenting herself to him.

He kissed a trail down her throat, his hands cupped around her breasts, squeezing, kneading. She gasped as he kissed her sensitive nipples, flicking his tongue against the hard little buds, making her shudder. All the while she felt the nearness of his cock at the opening of her sex, felt each little twitch and pulse as he drew out the moment. His willpower was astonishing; her own passion threatened to consume her.

"Take me," she gasped at last. "Please!"

But he clearly intended to savor every moment. His eyes shone with lust but he was still in control. Of himself and of her. It thrilled her. She writhed against him, pleading with her body, but his wicked smile told her who was master.

"My little wolf," he said, pinching her nipple, "at the mercy of her primal urges."

Madeleine gasped at the sweet pain. Every nerve in her body was wildly alive, wildly stimulated. She pictured herself at her master's feet, a chain around her neck. She would crouch beside his chair at the dining table and nibble morsels from his hand. And on those nights when the moon was full and she was too dangerous to be allowed to roam free, there was the cage.

His hand trailed over her breasts, down her belly and inner thighs and back up to where she wanted him most. He teased her slick folds, sliding his finger back and forth across the tiny knot of her clitoris. She gasped as pleasure jolted through her, down through her legs to her feet. His touch was like lightning, making her body leap and buck, setting her on fire.

She threw back her head with a cry as he pressed the flat of his hand up against her sex, moving it in slow, hard circles. Then he slipped a finger inside her. She felt it stroking the sensitive inner walls, exploring the warm wet center of her desire.

When he withdrew his hand she whimpered in protest. But he swatted her inner thighs, flooding her with excitement. She obeyed the silent instruction, spreading her legs as wide as they would go. She reached up to clutch the carved wooden headboard as he peeled her open with both hands, peering closely at her sex. When she felt his moist hot breath against her she trembled, but she kept herself splayed for him as he bent to kiss her, then to lick her.

The touch of his lips in so intimate a place was almost more than she could bear. If pain could be pleasure, then pleasure was also sometimes pain. She cried out with each little flick of his tongue against her most sensitive spot, and it was all she could do not to clamp her legs around his head. She shuddered with each violent spasm as he sent waves of stimulation throughout her body, manipulating her with his fingers as he kissed, licked, sucked her sleek, dewy folds.

When the climax came she screamed, thrashing wildly on the bed, her legs quaking with the shock waves of ecstasy. Her ears rang, howling with the inner wolf-voice that told her she wasn't finished, she wanted more, more, again, again....

And as though reading her thoughts, James at last angled his cock between her legs, sliding it inside her with one long, slow, excruciating thrust.

Her body still tingling with the aftershock of her orgasm, Madeleine clenched her inner muscles, wrapping her legs around him as she urged him deeper. He obliged, burying himself inside her. He slowly drew himself out, then pushed in, plunging inside her only to withdraw again. Each powerful thrust made her cry out and sent hot pulses through her entire body. Her climax seemed endless, a sensual assault that threatened to overwhelm her.

She gazed up at his muscular chest, his arms taut on either side of her as he held himself up. In his face were lust, love and fulfillment. All the passion she had craved and been deprived of by her husband, by society, by the nature of human beings who tortured themselves by denying the things they wanted most.

James panted with exertion as he fucked her, his own eyes blazing with animal wildness. Then he squeezed his eyes shut tightly, and his whole body went rigid as he came. Madeleine clung to him, gasping out his name and luxuriating in the sharp hot jets as he emptied himself into her.

Afterward they lay in a tangle of sweaty limbs, exhausted

and spent. Madeleine sighed with pleasure as James stroked her face, smoothing her tangled hair.

"You're breathtaking," he told her. "In both forms."

She blushed. It was strange to think that he had seen her secret other self, as though he'd glimpsed her naked and unaware. A wolf, a wild, beautiful wolf like those he kept in the zoo like treasured pets. How often she had admired them. How wonderful to know she was one of them.

An idea came to her as she studied James's features. His eyes were deep and dark, almost black, like his hair. He was a beautiful man, but as a wolf he would be magnificent. She imagined him in the forest with her, beneath the golden glow of the moon, running free and wild and held by no laws. Released once a month from the prison of their inferior human forms and allowed to become something more, something sublime.

And she smiled a secret little smile. When next the moon rose full and ripe, bringing with it the extraordinary change, she would bite him. She would make him like her. Then together they would pay a little visit to Henry, to reclaim what was hers.

"Where is your mind?" James asked wonderingly.

"With you," she said. "Forever."

Lightning in a Bottle

Kim Knox

My guardian had always thought me ignorant of the goings-on in his house.

A vapid girl, alone in the world, who never noticed the dark-robed men arriving in the dead of night. Who never wondered at the hints of sage and frankincense that drifted through the passages of his London townhouse in the early mornings. I knew, had known for quite some years that Henry Bellasis, Viscount Fauconberg, was a warlock. And now I knew that he planned to draw me into his world by offering my virginity to a stranger.

I wrapped my fingers around the great brass key, the pitted metal warming against my skin as I stood in the shadowed passage that led to the cellar door. The place where my guardian had bound his great secret.

Rumors from the footmen over the past week had run that Henry kept a dragon in the arched rooms that also housed his collection of metal automata. A great beast that steamed and groaned and licked fire into cook's little parlor when the wind blew north.

The maids shared darker stories as they made the beds or took a pan and brush to the ashes in the hearths. The dragon bound in the cellar did more than steam and groan. One maid had blushed scarlet and admitted in a rushed whisper that her dreams were full of a great, dark beast. A wicked beast...with a wicked mouth.

Not that I believed their tales. My guardian set himself up as a collector, an inventor, or that was the face he liked to present to the Fellows of the Royal Society. Those in his inner circle knew better. *I* knew better. There was no dragon in the cellar. There was something...darker.

I rubbed the key's bit, the sharp edge pressing into my thumb and digging a swift pain. I'd witnessed the rite that brought the creature into our world and now I stood with my heart almost in my throat, working to find the courage to push the key into the lock and turn it.

In the morning, my guardian would return from Sheffield with my betrothed. Another lie Henry expected me to believe. Aloysius Laythrop was a man more than twice my age, a steel-factory owner I had never met once in my life. However, he had a metal my guardian needed; therefore I was the quick payment for that deal.

I wet my lips and willed my heart to slow. A smile touched my mouth, and I felt the power of it. My guardian wouldn't have the chance to give my virginity to that man. I planned to offer it to someone else.

The grandfather clock chimed the quarter hour. Fifteen minutes until the stroke of midnight. So little time. The ceremony had begun then, with low chanting and the burning of frankincense.

I huffed out a breath, the air before me misting. Henry had

the license to decide whom I chose to marry by right of law, as I was not yet twenty-one, but he was using me for his own purposes. He cared little about any future with Mr. Aloysius Laythrop. Not that he *was* giving me a future. The promise of an engagement was a sham. My guardian had ruined more than one good woman, so why not his ward?

That made my decision for me.

The metal of the key clinked and clicked in the lock, and I held my breath. The house was silent, with only the familiar creaks of settling wood and the whistle of the winter wind down the chimney in cook's parlor. Nothing irregular. Nothing suggesting that one of the servants moved about the corridors.

The groan of the door hinges forced me to draw in a quick breath, my heart hammering in my chest. Chill air washed over me, scented with thyme. I swallowed. There was no choice in this. I could not allow Aloysius Laythrop to touch me.

I stepped across the threshold and lifted my lamp, my hand around the wooden handle damp with sweat. Shallow, golden light washed over the first few steps leading down into the thick, silent darkness.

Pressing my lips together to deny my need to call out into the silence, I pulled the door shut and locked it. Locked myself into the cellar. I had my guardian's only key, stolen from the secret compartment in his bureau. Nothing would disturb me. Nor stop me.

My bare feet were silent on the worn stone, the light brush of my chemise and the heavier cotton of my robe whispering behind me. The thought prickled my skin and I shivered. But still, I descended into the blackness.

The scent of thyme deepened, the added essences of rue and sage sliding across my thoughts. A week before those bewitching aromas had been deeper, thicker, lines of gray smoke enfolding the great open space of the cellar proper.

I don't know what drew me there on that night. A pull to my soul, perhaps. The right to see what would drive my guardian to sacrifice me to a stranger for a few ingots of metal. There were no great machines, no workbenches and tools in Henry's cellar. Yes he worked with metal, but in a way no other craftsman could. Fellows of the Royal Society thought they knew him, but they didn't know his inventions, the automata he displayed with such flourish, weren't wrought and fired by human hand.

Chanting had lifted to the high, arched ceiling with the heavy beat of male voices. My guardian stood in their midst, clad in flowing black silk, fire and liquid metal circling him in living spirals.

And seven days before he had called forth and bound his finest beast.

I stepped down from the last stair, the chill of the tiles shocking my feet. Light touched the first of Henry's inventions, carving out the shape of mechanical puppets varying in size, from a doll reaching to the height of my chin to automata rising a full head above me. My guardian displayed them with pride, had even shown them to the Queen herself. Lord Fauconberg was famed for them across all of London. They would totter over the floor, cogs and pistons whirring and chugging and snakes of steam streaming from their moving arms and legs.

They always churned the same smell. The sharp cut of coal and bitter smoke, as if a furnace burned at their heart.

I lifted my lamp to reveal the molded face of one of the automatons I remembered from my childhood. Possibly the first I had ever seen. Henry called him Romulus and there was the Roman harshness to his face, as if he'd been modeled on one of the busts of a great general. Romulus had always seemed so...real. Even with his unmoving mouth, iron chest and pistoned arms.

Offering a nervous smile to his blank face, I lowered my lamp and moved on, weaving through the rows of automata. Light glimmered over their progression, from the almost crude mechanics of Romulus to the growing smoothness, the way joints eased into a more natural form, until only the shine of enameled steel gave away their true nature.

Henry never displayed these later models. They stayed safely in the cellars for his own enjoyment. He called them his menagerie. A dark grin would follow and he'd murmur that there was nothing so precious to him as his lightning caught in so many bottles.

I stopped at the first ring carved into the floor. The automata circled it, their blank faces turned into the wide space it marked. Sigils cut the ring's perfection, the dried flake of blood catching the lamplight. Two more circles wound inward to the high stone oblong of a bare altar...and to the creature who stood beside it. In the wild rite that had created him, Henry had declared his name Augustus.

My heart tightened and the lamp rattled in my hand as my nerves stretched.

I had watched that creation. Crouched at the top of the stairs, I'd witnessed the fire and steel whirl up from the concentric circles and form his perfection. Though he still wore bare steel, Augustus was a silvered man in every detail. My gaze moved over his body, and my breath caught. *Every* detail.

I straightened my shoulders, willing courage. This silvered man was the most practical solution to my problem. A touch of a smile lifted my mouth. Offering myself to him was also a sharp poke at my guardian. Let one of his creatures have what he wanted to give away so freely. Something twisted under that thought, something deeper that I didn't want to examine too closely. Denying that urge forced me to speak.

"Great Augustus, I come to offer myself to you."

The words had a hollow turn to them in the heavy silence of the cellar and I waited, my pulse drumming and my stomach in a knot. The press of the automata surrounded me, so close the scent of steel was in my every breath.

"Rebecca Marwood."

A shiver ran over my skin as my name whispered through the air. My guardian's creations never spoke. Never. The first true thud of fear dropped into my belly...but I couldn't retract my offer. I knew that much about magic. I was committed now.

"You offer yourself. Why?"

I lifted my chin, holding Augustus's blank, unmoving gaze. The firm, powerful voice could belong to no one else. "Lord Fauconberg plans to give me to Aloysius Laythrop in return for seven ingots. For a metal that concerns you. I believe my plan can benefit us both."

Augustus's low laughter skittered through my flesh. "So practical, Rebecca." His head tilted, the slow slide of metal blooming heat in my chest. "Now tell me the true reason."

Honesty. He wanted something I could barely admit to myself. I wet my lips. "I saw your creation."

Augustus blinked, the soft rasp of metal against metal, and stayed silent. Waiting.

"And...I saw what you did."

"Rebecca..." His voice wrapped around my name, low and deep and igniting a little pulse of unexpected warmth in my belly. "If you cannot give me your truth, then we can have no pact."

The images of what I'd witnessed burned against my closed eyelids. Lady Saunders, one of Henry's inner circle, found her robes removed by the smooth hands of automata, and naked, she lay on the altar. Augustus, his silver skin gleaming and new, had slid his hands over her white thighs, parting them. With one thrust, he had buried himself within her, her spine arching and a violent gasp of pleasure escaping her lips.

The rhythmic thrust of his hips had burned heat up through my own flesh, shortened my breath and pushed an unknown ache between my thighs. Only the break in the chant of the robed men had brought me back to myself. I fled the cellar, but the memory burned...and my guardian's threat gave me the opportunity to play out my forbidden desire.

My heart in my mouth, I admitted the truth. "I wanted to lie in Lady Saunders's place. For you to have me, not her."

A smile pulled at Augustus's mouth, the steel mask moving as easily as flesh. "Then come forward."

I willed my body to move, stepping over the first thick ring. A flare of warmth ran over my calves like a whisper of breath, stirring my nightclothes.

One of the automata moved to stand in front of me before I reached the second ring. I stared up at him, finding a dark smile on his mouth. His fingers moved to the laces and buttons of my robe, untying and slipping them through with ease. Another automaton took the lamp from my hand, a third drawing the robe from my shoulders.

Cool fingers teased down my bare arms before the three slipped away to join the circle of automata beyond the first ring. The scent of thyme hung still in the air. I moved forward again, crossing the second ring, the rush of heat like hot hands on my thighs. I sucked in a quick breath, ignoring the burst of fear. I wanted this. I held Augustus's hard gaze. I wanted *him*.

Another automaton stood before me. His cool hands cupped my shoulders, his thumbs tugging at the straps of my chemise. My heart thudded. I wore nothing beneath.

The automaton held my gaze, a strange dark light firing in the depths of his eyes. With only a slight tug, his steel thumbs cut through the bands of cotton. His hands moved, drawing the material down, cupping my breasts and pulling a gasp from me. My flesh felt heavy, pulsing, hardly my own as his cool thumbs stroked over my nipples. And still he drew away the chemise, exposing my skin to the watching automata.

The air hummed around me and I bit my lip as his large hands slid over my hips, his thumbs so close to my aching center that I had to fight the urge to twist and turn into his fleeting touch.

But then he was gone...a shadow disappearing into the waiting crowd. And they *were* waiting. The feel of them whispered against my skin, but I could only look to Augustus.

Want burned from him. "Cross the third ring, Rebecca."

Had Lady Saunders felt like this? Her body thick and heavy with a need she could hardly recognize, the anticipation of what was to come hot in her flesh?

I stepped forward over the third ring and the heat of ghostly hands slipped over my body, sliding between my legs. A low moan broke from me as sweet heat flashed under my skin, and I put out a hand to the altar to steady myself.

Augustus lifted an eyebrow. "You come to me more ready than Lady Saunders. Though her, these evenings have become more of a...chore."

"What...what do I do?"

Augustus looked beyond me and the stir of air and thyme

said the menagerie moved silently across the rings. Cool, metal hands skimmed my shoulders, my hips, and my pulse jumped, a squeak escaping me as they lifted me from the floor. They laid me over strong arms and yet more fingers drifted over my belly, my breasts, dipping tantalizingly between my thighs to stroke and finding hidden points that fired pure pleasure.

I stared up, shadows chasing over their painted faces. They seemed so...alive, dark heat burning over me from their fierce gazes. Their touch hummed over and through me as hands parted my thighs. Smooth fingers dug into my flesh and my heart pounded, a need I could barely name thick and hot in my belly.

The cold stone of the altar was a shock to my skin...and then Augustus's hands pushed over my calves, knees, thighs, more man than metal with a rough heat that drummed my pulse. He drew me toward him as the automata released me until I lay supine across the altar staring up at Augustus.

"You didn't...Lady Saunders..."

"We would not gift her with such attention." His hips brushed against my damp thighs, the steel of his body warm and almost rough to the touch. He ran light fingers across my skin to tease over my belly. "She is far from deserving."

I swallowed. "And I am?"

He held my gaze, points of dark fire in the depths of his eyes now. "You desire this. You desire *me*. And you offer me"—he looked up briefly to the automata—"offer *us* a treasure." His thumb stole between my thighs, languid and sure. I groaned, my chest tight as he licked his thumb. "A blood virgin of the man who bound us." His smile was dark. "It's little wonder he wants you finally covered by some gnarled old man.

"With you taken, he planned to call on no more of our

kind." Augustus stroked over my thighs, so close to where I ached for him. "He taunted us with you."

"With me?"

The fingers of the automata returned to stroke over my arms and linger over the curves of my breasts, rolling my nipples between slow fingers. The thrill of it wove pleasure down to my belly.

"He gave us others down the years. But you were sweeter bait, promised to my brethren for almost a year now. A promise that drew me here too."

His hardness pushed against me, flickering heat under my skin and with it the instinct to push, to find the joy he offered. Augustus watched me, his eyes pure fire. "I will take you as you deserve to be taken."

He gripped my thighs, his silver hands gleaming against my pale skin and eased his hips forward. Pain sliced through me and I shut my eyes against it, denying the mewl that wanted to break free. Smooth automata hands gripped mine, yet more stroking over my shoulders and under my breasts, the hum of their metal flesh easing the slow cut of agony.

"Look at me, Rebecca."

I opened my eyes to the fire in his. Their intensity held me. "I..."

"You belong to us. To *me*."

He thrust and buried himself within me. I cried out, arching against his sudden invasion. Tears blurred my eyes, but light fingertips wiped them from my cheek and smooth metal lips brushed my temple.

"*Ours.*"

The whisper—the soft beat of so many voices within it— washed over my skin.

Augustus drew back, the friction of his metal flesh against mine hot and fierce. "You are perfection. Truly." He pushed forward again and I met him, driving him deeper, wanting him, the memory of his hard, fast thrusts too clear in my thoughts.

The altar beneath me groaned and Augustus's grin was wickedness itself. "Yes." The single word was a growl and his hands dug into my thighs, driving himself again into my body.

Sharp altar stone cut into my back, bringing with it a brief flare of pain before it and the stone crumbled away. Strong hands held me as I flailed, urging me up until I grabbed Augustus's hard shoulders. I clung to him, my thighs hard around his hips and him firm and wanted within me. Need raged and I ached for him to move again, to fire pleasure through my body and make me his.

His breath misted with mine, the fire in his gaze white with heat. "We were his menagerie. Caught and held for his exhibition." His lips brushed my mouth. "Though you were equally caged." His hands cupped my backside, fingers teasing into the cleft and I moaned. My lips slid over his, unsure and wanting, and he briefly took my bottom lip between his teeth. His grin was equally sharp. "Time to set us all free."

His mouth took mine, his tongue curling, dueling, and I clung to him, moving with the rhythms he set. Fire flickered up my spine as other mouths and fingers played and kissed and licked my skin.

I cried out as a hot tongue darted between my cleft, driving me down hard against Augustus. He grinned at me, something wild and wanton. "We would all enjoy you, Rebecca. It's our way."

"Who... What..." My words broke as the tongue pushed deeper, the flare of hot rapture spiraling up through my flesh and dancing light before my eyes. "Dear God in heaven!"

Augustus smirked and thrust deep. "Not quite."

The tongue found a rhythm with Augustus's strokes, and I simply fell into the passion of so many mouths and fingers on my body, of Augustus taking me, my flesh pushing hard against the growing heat of his. The rub of my breasts, my belly over his roughened skin drove me to find his mouth for myself, to demand deep, hot kisses, to draw groans from him and a faster, harder stroke into my needy flesh.

Fire danced within me, wreathes of it coiling tighter and tighter in my belly. I shook, but firm hands held me, moved me. Augustus broke his mouth from mine and I pressed my face to the crook of his neck.

His lips burned against my ear. "Let go, Rebecca. Let us take you completely."

"Yes." I groaned the word against his softened skin. "I want them. I want *you*."

His teeth grazed my earlobe and the pain skittered into sharp pleasure. "You have us. And we will have you." The promise tightened my flesh almost to the point of pain. "Forever."

Hot waves of molten fire smashed over me and I cried out, the light, the fierce passion sweeping away my thoughts as Augustus still thrust into my body, harder and faster, deepening my wild joy. His own body stiffened and a long, low moan escaped him. For an endless moment, he buried his face in my loose hair and the touch of the others faded back, leaving only us two.

His trembling hand touched my cheek and he dropped a warm kiss onto my dazed mouth. "Such perfection," he murmured.

The hands of the automata returned and drew me away

from Augustus, pulling me back through the rings to their very edge. My heart turned over. He had *promised*—

His smile was dark, the silver shine to his skin fading even as I stared. Cracks spidered over his arms, his broad chest, running down across his hips to his legs. Fire churned beneath, making the black lines molten. What was happening? Was it something I'd done? He'd promised, but those cracks didn't mean forever. I tried to wrench myself free of the hands that held me, but they were unyielding.

And then Augustus simply...shattered.

I screamed and strong hands held me up as my knees buckled. My vision darkened, and I fought not to faint. What had I *done*? My desire for Augustus had destroyed him.

"Rebecca..." His voice swept over the drone in my ears. It was low...and amused. "Look at me."

I shook my head to clear my thoughts. In the center of the floor, a floor clear of rings and blood and sigils, stood Augustus. But he was no longer encased in steel. His skin held an earthy, reddish hue and great wings grew from his back to brush the curve of the brick ceiling. In the flickering lamplight, I spied the slim flick of a forked tail.

"Do you fear me?"

He was a demon. Henry had trapped a spirit from hell itself. And I should have feared that, but it wasn't terror thrumming through my blood and making my heart pound. I'd wanted him from the moment I saw him. I didn't care from whence he came.

I swallowed and pushed against the hands holding me. They drifted away. I smiled and on unsure feet, I closed the distance between us to stand before him. Nervous fingers tracing a slow line down his broad chest. He was hot, his skin smooth, and under my palm I found the heavy thud of his beating heart.

Augustus closed his eyes and a trail of thyme-scented smoke curled from his mouth. His tail curled around my thigh and teased a fresh run of pleasure under my skin.

The sudden hiss of air around me, sweeping warmth across the floor, forced me to look away and I found the cellar empty. "They're like you?"

"To a degree." He held my gaze, his eyes alive with a golden fire. His lips twisted into a wicked smile. "A *lesser* degree."

My cheeks reddened and nerves pulled at me again. I began to doubt his promise. The menagerie had flown free of the cage my guardian had built around them. "Tell me what you are." I needed to know, so that when he left the memory of our time together could warm me. And he *would* vanish. He was a demon. Doubt said that he would never keep his word. "What did Henry want with you?"

He curled a damp strand of my hair around his finger. "We are Antanelis." His voice was deep and achingly soft. The need to melt into it, to press myself against him, feel the beat of his heart under my cheek seared through me. I resisted. "Warlocks trap us for amusement. For proof of their power and skill."

"You're lightning in a bottle."

"Yes. Simply that."

I glanced back to the empty cellar. "For so many years." I pressed a light kiss to his heart, closing my eyes as the scent of his skin threaded through me. Demon or not, no one deserved such torture. "I'm sorry."

He tilted my chin to brush my lips with his, the lingering hint of thyme wrapping around my tightening heart. I kept my eyes closed, desperate not to witness his leaving. He'd given me a kiss of good-bye.

"You promised me a place with you." The words escaped me and I winced. I was being silly, stupid. The vapid girl Henry thought me. No, I had to be practical. "Of course, you don't have to honor..."

"Rebecca." His shadowed grin was lascivious as he pressed his hot hands to my hips. His tail dipped between the wetness of my thighs and my pulse jumped. "I will *always* have a place for you."

The warmth and softness of his wings enfolded me and with his kiss warming my lips, we vanished from my guardian's house.

THE WILDEST SPIRIT

Sacchi Green

C oyotes howled at the cold white eye of the moon, igniting a deeper howl low in the man's throat. He fought it down, resisted the damp autumn earth tugging at his feet, the maze of scents coiling from the shadows.

"I promised you they'd sing." She stood silhouetted in the doorway, her blanket spread wide so that its shadow reached out across him like great wings while her warm, demanding scent enfolded him.

Impossible to guess how much she understood. If she *knew...* He had killed for that. But not this time.

The thought of flesh on flesh, of smooth arms and slim, strong legs, drew him toward her. Even now, with the moon and the cool, dark forest calling to him like a home he'd never known, her human body kept him still in man-form.

He had sensed the danger since their first chance meeting. In one of his biology courses at the university there was talk of coyotes moving into resurgent wilderness at the eastern edge of the valley, so one day, on impulse, he drove into the hills to look for signs.

Not far along a gated logging road an approaching horse and rider made him turn abruptly back. Even in man-form his effect on horses could be, at best, unpredictable.

The hoofbeats quickened. Before he reached his car the mare had cut him off, and his growl, too low for human ears, did no more than send a shiver across her chestnut hide.

The University Police insignia on the saddle blanket explained it. This horse was trained for steadiness even among drunken, rioting students. Well trained, and well handled. He looked up at the rider.

She had no special claim on grace or beauty. Her tawny hair, tied back for comfort, was pleasing without intent or artifice. So why this sudden sense of danger?

Even through the mellow, meaty warmth of horseflesh the woman's scent called to him, enticing, demanding. He had known many women, some beautiful, some brave, some seeking to destroy him; and he had known that the pleasure they offered would never be more than fleeting. This one could be no different.

He tried to subdue the wolf-senses, but it was too late. And she was sublimely unaware...or did some flickering reaction cross her face?

If so, it was gone at once. She wore no uniform, but carried authority in her bearing and her clear gray eyes.

"Hold it right there, please."

He was done with orders, even in a voice that sent ripples across his skin. He moved back a step or two to ease the mare and then began to circle toward his car.

She urged the skittish horse forward. "Don't be an idiot. I've got twelve-hundred pounds between my legs."

He glanced at the long slim jeans gripping the horse's flanks, and then, with one dark eyebrow raised, looked up into her face.

Her official stance wavered. She struggled to suppress a grin. "Sorry. Forget I said that. I'd just appreciate it if you'd let me inspect your car."

"Sure." He tossed her the keys. She dismounted and then, still holding the reins, searched briefly but professionally through his car and trunk.

"Forestry students raising marijuana in the clearings?"

"I wish that were all. Somebody's been setting out traps and poisoned bait for the coyotes. You're anxious to leave, and wearing camouflage; it seemed worth checking out."

"The clothes are army leftovers. I've only been a civilian for six months."

"Sorry. I take this coyote-killing too personally. I live near here, and it feels like a violation of my territory."

Coyote-killing. A smoldering rage heated his veins. Wolves in a pack would kill coyotes to wipe out competition for their prey, but that men should do so, and with traps and poison, was something else entirely.

The mare tossed her head and half reared. Had he growled aloud? The rider shot him a startled look as she mounted and brought the horse under control.

The man-voice came with an effort. "I take it personally, too." She stared into his narrowed eyes, nodded, wheeled and let the horse move swiftly away up the trail.

Fury wrestled with fear. Fury at the killings; fear at the lure of the woman's scent.

He changed deliberately that night. The moon showed only three-fourth's full, but he had long ago learned to change at will.

In the forest blood called him, though he had no honest hunger; he killed and fed for pleasure, like a man, and felt shame, like a man, and hoped a bloody muzzle would curb the urge to seek out the woman where she slept.

The coyote pack watched from a distant hillside, assessing the danger, noting that he was only a solitary hunter. They shared with him a wide and subtle range of cues and signals, but to ask of traps and poison, offer help, was beyond him.

Which brought him back to the woman. As all thoughts brought him back to the woman, even while a separate part of his mind kept on with his studies at the university.

His army pension was enough for subsistence, and he had not always ignored the opportunities for extra income that came with covert operations. It would have been easy to find work as a mercenary, but he had done enough killing under the dubious justification of service to country. It had come too close to turning him into an "animal" of a kind that had nothing to do with the wolf. No more killing under orders.

What he wanted from education was a different perspective on humanity. What he wanted was a reason better than lust not to abandon the man-form altogether.

Which brought his thoughts again to the woman. He knew her house, had seen the horse trailer there that first day. The mare, luckily, was stabled on campus in the valley. It took three days to find the woman at home in daylight; night, he told himself, ignoring the press of the inevitable, was out of the question.

She tensed in recognition. "Yes?"

"I can find the coyote killer." He thrust a thick envelope into her hands. "Special ops. Tracking skills, night-movement training. Look through my papers, military discharge, citations, health records, before you decide whether to trust me." Much of it was lies, but the army's lies, not his own. She leafed automatically through the papers, then paused at the health records.

She was not, after all, unaware.

"Ten months ago, negative," he said. "No one since." The HIV and STD testing had amused him at the time, made him wonder what they might find in his blood if only they knew how to look.

"Three years," she said, meeting his eyes, a slight flush spreading from throat to face. Then, scarcely skipping a beat, "I'll show you where I've found the traps."

They walked along the logging road together. The top of her head came only to his eyes, but her stride matched his; he was keenly conscious of her long legs.

She turned onto a narrow trail among white birches. He was aware as always of the texture of the forest, the sounds and scents; aware too that she observed him, assessed him. Three years! No wonder she felt the pull.

He had always avoided any females perceptive enough to be dangerous. The world still offered plenty of silly, blankly pretty faces, but it was harder and harder to feel any interest in them.

Now he walked with a woman through a forest as much her world as his, one who was neither silly nor pretty, but utterly compelling. And dangerous.

"There was a trap here, and poisoned meat farther along."

He smelled recent death.

"There were at least two other places, half a mile or so from here. I've cleared it all away, turned in the traps, so he must know I'm watching."

"'He?' Just one?"

"I think so. I have pretty good tracking skills myself, but I'm open to a second opinion."

Wolf-sense tested the air while human eyes took in visual details. He moved along the path, then off to one side, finding where the poison had lain.

"Yes, one alone."

She took him to other roads, other trails. "The same one." He would know that foulness now at a mile or more with the wind in the right quarter.

"This is university land, for forestry research, but there's not enough manpower to patrol here. I search out the traps on my own time. The coyotes may be learning, and he may have given up, but damn! I want to get him!"

Beneath her savage expression he was startled to see tears. "If you had seen...I had to finish one off myself out of mercy. A cub. Maybe that's why I'm mad enough to think of sending an ex-commando into the night woods."

"There's no way you could stop me."

Her eyes glinted. He tried to defuse the challenge. "No weapons. Not even a knife. You could search me before I go."

The glint in her eyes was of laughter now. "How could I turn down an offer like that?" She moved back down the trail, her scent, movements, swaying hair, the rhythm of long legs and curving hips, promising everything. The place and moment were her own to choose.

They were close enough to the paved road to hear passing cars when suddenly she stopped. He pushed on until his body pressed against hers. A flock of wild turkeys was crossing their path; he should have sensed them sooner, but his blood was pounding to other rhythms than the hunt.

The woman was silent, her body language clear as her hips

moved against his urgent pressure. When he bent to nuzzle her neck she reached behind to grip his flanks and force him even harder into her softness.

Then she pulled away, leaving a cold ache where her heat had been. The turkeys scattered and flapped up into the branches.

In the car he touched her knee, stroked slowly up her thigh and then down again. She kept her eyes on the road, just a hint of unsteadiness in her voice. "Saturday is the full moon. The coyotes will yip and howl at the moon and each other. You should come to hear them."

Wait three days? Impossible, and her body knew it as well as his. Just as they came to the house she reached out and traced a searing path along his inner thigh that jolted him like lightning.

Then she was in the house, stripping off her sweater, unbuckling her belt, all without speaking, without turning.

He kicked the door shut and fumbled at his boots. By the time he got to the bedroom door she was kneeling naked on the bed, loosened hair streaming down around her face.

He knelt behind her and she pressed back, guiding him, drawing him into her own hunger, her own rhythm. The only sound was her quickening breathing, and his, and the brush of hair across her shoulders as her head twisted from side to side until at last a cry burst from her so keen and piercing that he never knew whether his own cries came in the man's voice or the wolf's.

They slept, and woke, and she leaned above him with a wildness beyond beauty, rousing him to new dimensions of the human body's joys, then to pleasures a dream-like step beyond. There came a timeless moment when, her body riding his, her head thrown back in that shrill, triumphant cry, the solid earth dropped away and they plummeted together through space.

Falling, falling, cold air ripping past, battering them, forcing the ecstasy deeper and deeper, holding it there, unending.... Until at last a great sweep of wings brought darkness, and oblivion.

He did not go into the forest that night.

In the morning she kissed the furrows her nails had carved in his shoulders, stroked the silver streaks in his black hair lightly, almost shyly, then armored herself in a uniform and left for the campus. She had asked nothing of him, but he wrote *Saturday* in coffee grounds across her kitchen counter.

Along the road he checked the entrances to all the trails she'd shown him. No new scent. He drove to campus himself and endured a class or two.

Back in the woods that night he knelt on springy hemlock needles, clearing his mind, reaching out to the night-scented air. Muscles, tendons, thoughts shifted, adjusted. The black pelt and the plumed tail were the greatest energy drain; all else was largely rearrangement.

The forest revealed no traps, no poison, no coyotes nearer than the next ridge. He let the cool essence of northern woods overlay the fevered jungle that still erupted into his dreams and left the taste of human blood on his tongue. Morning had begun to tint the hills by the time he returned to his car and clothing and drove down into the valley.

As Saturday dawned the black wolf lay in thick brambles, his unblinking amber stare fixed on the house across the clearing. It was just past sunrise when she came out, swung an ax, split wood, stacked it, and the hidden watcher feared the change would overwhelm him, so intense was the need to feel that lithe body against his own flesh.

As soon as she had taken her load of wood indoors the wolf crept deeper into the shadows and then loped toward the place where his clothes were cached. Minutes later the man was at her door.

By evening, at the rise of the full moon, he watched the woman doze before the fire. They had traveled far that day, miles by car and on foot over woods roads and trails, farther still sharing inner paths.

She knew more now than he had understood himself before opening to her. The military life had saved him, just barely, from the self-destructive wildness of his youth, but distant bureaucracies had used his talents for purposes he neither understood nor shared. There had been a price, one he was still paying.

The essential secret of his nature he kept hidden, but she might have guessed, might have understood without believing. He couldn't tell. For all her openness, all the sharing of her own lonely life, she had depths still hidden from him. And for all the meeting of minds, of emotions, the physical urgency still overwhelmed all else and there, at least, nothing was held back.

That night he enjoyed the play of firelight over her naked curves and valleys, even as the wolf's uneasiness with flames kept him on edge.

The moon rose higher and whiter in the sky. When the first coyote call pierced the darkness he pulled on jeans and a shirt and escaped into the clear, cold night.

It was then, when in spite of the call of the night and the moon he found himself back in her embrace, twining his own legs in the silken length of hers, that he began to think there might be no escape.

But she twisted away with a laugh. "No, not yet, just listen to them sing. It makes me want to howl with them." And he allowed himself the brief dream that there might be some alternative to escape or destruction.

Over the next few weeks they searched the forest together and singly, destroying a few more traps, learning more about their quarry, but coming no closer to him.

Another full moon approached. There would be a total eclipse this time, a sight he had last glimpsed through a jungle canopy. The memory of that dull red eye brought dreams that shocked him awake in her bed, sweating, trembling, dazed to find himself in man-form. She offered silent comfort, asking nothing.

He was relieved, but puzzled, even disappointed, that she asked so little. She would listen, but never probe; she freely showed her joy in him but never asked as he left when or whether he would come again.

They never talked of anything but an abstract future. The closest she came was to say, as they watched the sunrise together, "You should see dawn in the mountains, above the tree line, when the valleys below are filled with cloud and the sky above is clear to infinity. There's nothing more real than that, just stone and space and the coming of light over the edge of the world."

Not, "Come with me someday to see…" Only, "You should see…" At least he knew now where she carried him on those surges of ecstasy. He had fallen with her through that space, that light, past those sheer stone cliffs. He might be beginning to sense, without truly believing, her essential nature.

On the day of the eclipse, the drifting fog tasted of death. She knew by his tension as they started up the trail. When she crouched beside the grimacing carcass he stopped her with a snarl.

"Get away!" The harshness came from rage and guilt, and his need to be alone before the change overcame him. Mist swirled between them as she tried to read his face. He avoided her eyes, focusing on the blood-red barberries, the tufts of gray fur caught on the thorny bush in the coyote's death convulsions.

"Leave it! I…" The man-voice came with an effort. "I should have been here. If you hadn't kept me…"

Blaming her couldn't ease his guilt. While the young coyote lay dying, the man and woman had been forcing the boundaries of pleasure and pain, pushing tension to extremes until they were swept over the edge. His flesh still resonated to the memory, even as bones and tendons screamed to lengthen, shorten, change.

"Get away! Leave me alone!"

She straightened, arms clutched around her belly as though to keep herself from shaking. Wide gray eyes burned through the fog.

"Yes. It's time. I never meant to keep you, never expected…" Then she was gone, but a last whisper drifted to him on a streamer of mist: "Good-bye, and thank you." He blocked it out.

The wolf crouched in the underbrush through the day, a black hole masked by swirling cloud. Toward evening the air cooled and cleared; sunset glowered in the west as the moon rose in the east.

He waited. Coyotes circled at a distance. Condensation soaked his outer fur, but the heat at his core burned steady and intense.

The earth's shadow crept across the moon, and across his mind. Only a bright sliver of clarity remained when tires crunched on gravel by the gate a quarter mile away, and the scent he awaited trickled toward him on a faint breeze.

To keep the wolf-form was to commit to a kill. In man-form, capture would still be an option. But something in him fought the change, and then, as he pressed, he knew with a touch of panic that it wasn't going to happen.

He thought of the woman, mouth against mouth, skin against naked skin, but words stabbed through his mind; *I never meant to keep you... Good-bye...*

The moon was a dull red bruise. Old images throbbed inside his skull; another darkened moon, other deaths, blood-scent saturating the thick jungle air; another failed attempt to change.

Coyote voices cut through his clouded thoughts. A few adolescent yips at first, then howls, then the full voice of the pack-leader not far away. The wolf focused, committed, let his rage feed on the reek of fear and hatred spilling from the killer.

Another howl, closer now, and the man slowed his approach. The acid stink of his fear seared the air. He stopped, and the wolf tensed to pursue, but another howl from behind drove the man forward.

A light wavered, glinting on a long knife and the dull steel of a rifle barrel.

With what remained of man-thought the wolf wondered what dark fantasy drove the killer, what madness impelled him through darkness and terror, hating the coyotes, fearing them, without reason. Even wolves were too sane to waste effort on revenge.

Except for this wolf.

The killer came on again, the beam of his light sweeping the brushy roadside. It swung past the wolf, stopped, swung back.

In the absence of weapons he would have taken time to savor the man's terror. Only a second now to display slanted eyes blazing with reflected light; then a snarl, just enough for the flash of teeth longer than any coyote's; then, as the light crashed to the ground and the gun swung forward, a twisting leap that carried him under and to the right of the burst of gunfire. A strong, smashing shoulder; the man, unbalanced already by the gun's recoil and his own panic, went down with a guttural scream.

The wolf was on him, slashing the forearm that clutched the rifle, snapping the bones with powerful jaws. The man still gripped the knife in his other hand, but the wolf scarcely felt it slice his thigh. The scent of his own blood was a mere trickle in the hot flood that swept him as he tore through the man's shoulder, face, throat. Human blood in his nostrils, his mouth, his gullet, blood not just of this human but all those others, under that other bloody moon, as his comrade lay dying on the jungle floor and the wolf-form had no hands to help him, carry him, no voice to radio for help, no human thought but the thirst for vengeance.

This man died too easily. Only that fleeting thought linked the wolf to the remnants of his own humanity.

A bright crescent rimmed the moon's dark bruise. The wolf moved, stiffly at first, then at a limping trot, crossing a stream where the torrent flushed the blood from his coat and cleaned his wound. The slash was shallow, since thick fur had obstructed the blade, but movement kept the wound bleeding and he would eventually weaken.

He needed a den, a safe place to rest and heal, but his sense of place wavered as the woods around him warped into twisted, reeking jungle, reverted to northern forest, then distorted again.

Emerging into a clearing he saw, by the light of the half-restored moon, the haven where instinct had led him. He crept toward the house and the moon-washed figure waiting. The rightness of it drew him; the wrongness dragged at him and kept him low to the ground.

She reached a hand out slowly. He growled a warning. *No human touch!* But this touch, so familiar...

She backed gradually up the steps to the door and then into the lamp-lit interior. He followed, stiff-legged, unable to either close the distance or let it lengthen.

Slowly, slowly she sank to the floor. Her eyes closed, freed him from the painful intensity of her gaze. She fumbled at her shirt collar, swept back her hair, and arched her smooth, vulnerable throat in symbolic submission.

He crept forward, tested her with jaws that pressed gently from nape to windpipe. Then he released her neck and lay his dark head against her shoulder, drawing in her scent in great shuddering sighs as her arms went around him and a cloud of russet hair fell forward to mingle with night-black fur.

At last she leaned back enough to stroke the silver streaks at his temples. Traces of shock still showed on her face, but more than a trace of tenderness.

Then her hand moved carefully toward his wounded thigh, and her touch set off such ripples of pleasure that he almost missed the signals of impending change.

She stiffened at his urgent growl. He thrust his muzzle against her eyes to keep them closed, then tried to pull away.

Her arms tightened. He gave in, let the change surge through his body as her voice flowed over him, murmuring, comforting. "It's all right, all right, all right." Her hands and body clung to his as the wolf-form became man-form.

At last he lay naked and exhausted in her arms. With an effort he raised a hand to open her eyes. The man-voice came with an effort. "You knew?"

"Not *knew*. Just wanted. I thought it was my private fantasy."
She stroked his head again, then moved her hand down over
shoulder, chest, belly. When she eased from under him to kneel
by his side and lower her face toward his loins a surge of longing
stirred him, but her mouth went to his wounded thigh. Gently
she licked away the blood.

"Your blood...could it make me..."

"No," he said. "You have to be born to it." And she wasn't,
she couldn't be, he would have known if that flesh had ever
changed. But there was still something unfathomable, something infinitely strange and wild about her.

"I thought so." The shadow crossing her face went far
beyond disappointment. She tossed the hair out of her face and
stood. "He's dead?"

It took him a moment to understand. "Yes."

"Your clothes are near there?"

"Yes. I'll have to get them." He started to rise, wavered,
then made it to the couch.

"It's my turn now." She shrugged into a jacket. "Will it look
as though coyotes did it?"

"Coyotes couldn't." The crack of a heavy arm bone between
his jaws echoed in his head.

"We can't let them be blamed, hunted down. And talk of a
wolf would be even worse." She felt in a pocket and drew out
gloves. "Is the knife that cut you still out there?"

He nodded, and was swept by a wave of dizziness. She
seemed to know what she was doing.

It was at least an hour before he heard her car return.
When she didn't come in he went out, wrapped in a blanket.
She sat stiff and silent, the light of the clear full moon slanting
across her staring face, her hands clenched so tightly on the

steering wheel that he had to pry them loose.

Gently he eased her out of the car, but she struggled so violently that he let her go. Then she began to retch. All he could do was to steady her and smooth her hair back and try to warm her in the blanket.

At last, long after there was nothing left to come up, she staggered up the steps, tearing at her clothes as she went.

"Inside out...so I wouldn't stain the car." He helped her strip, then subdued the inner wolf and built up the fire so that it would consume her gore-smeared clothes. Her gloves were beyond belief.

"It's all right now. Only a human could...they'll call it insanity, madness." She was retching out a stream of words. "The knife, over and over, down to the bones, over and over. But it's all right now."

He held her tightly while she shook, tried to warm her, carried her at last to the shower to wash the blood and cold from her body. When he had her wrapped in a fresh blanket and seated before the fire he tried to get some solid information.

"Where is the knife now?"

She stared into the flames. "In his heart. In a tree."

"I'm not sure I understand."

"The knife," she answered patiently, "is sticking through his heart and into a tree, as high up as I could reach. The rest of him...well, no one will think a coyote, or wolf, had anything to do with it."

He steeled himself against the impulse to shrink away, even as the wolf within recognized that she was right, and wise, and braver in her own wild way than he could ever be.

Her calm was fleeting. She began to shake again, arms

clutched around her belly, and he tried to soothe her with hands and words.

"You did what you had to do, it *will* be all right. You did it for them, for me."

"Not for you." Her words came in a raw, exhausted whisper. He felt a tendril of cold fog brush his face and heard other whispered words; *I never meant to keep you...*

"I couldn't have done it just for you. I would have tried, but I couldn't have done it."

"What, then?"

Her voice became gradually steadier. "I never meant to tell you, to ask anything of you, never expected you to stay. I didn't realize how much I would want you to stay. I just knew that I wanted you, even more than I wanted what you could give me."

Scent had told him, instinct had told him, but his brain had shut them out because it was supposed to be impossible.

"I'm not asking you to stay with me even now." She turned from the fire at last and her gray eyes were deep and fierce. In the flickering light he seemed to see the shadow of great wings.

"You don't have to stay, but *be* there, be somewhere I can reach, because now that I *know*, I will not be left to raise this child alone."

He started to ask, "Do you *want* me to stay?" then said, instead, "There's no way you can keep me from staying." She dropped the blanket and pressed against him with such fervor that the unasked question was answered.

He would have to tell her someday that only changers could breed with changers, even though her wild spirit might never break free of human-form.

Wolf-bone to man-bone was a small step, full pelt to sparsely furred skin and a thick head of hair only a matter of degree. But mammal-bone to air-chambered hawk-bone, hair to feathers, arms to wings...

He had never heard of such a leap, never imagined it until she carried him in ecstasy to the high, clear realm of the hawk and slashed the sky in the falcon's mating dive.

What child would come from the blending of his blood with her far stranger, wilder spirit? He was afraid to even wonder. But he would be there.

Blood Soup

Benji Bright

Jasper Roux set down the beaten leather pack on the beaten wooden counter and he unrolled his knives. Each of his twelve knives was sharp, but there's nothing miraculous about a sharp knife alone. These knives—from the slim sliver of iron with a fine bone handle to the crooked butcher knife with its stained oak grip—each of them told a story in Jasper's hands. Between the fingers of a master, they sang.

The kitchen was cold when Jasper entered, the daytime chef having left it over an hour before and the house staff forbidden from entering between the shifts of the two men like children pressed between the stormy whims of their parents. Jasper did not mind the cold. Old houses had their drafts and Echo Manor was the oldest.

He lit the lamps and fired the stoves himself. He liked to feel the grain and heft of the pieces of wood between his fingers before he fed them to the fire. He selected the best, hardiest logs, cut daily by the outdoor servants. Once the kitchen began to warm, the kitchen staff began to enter. They deferred to him and kept their eyes low, busying themselves with those mundane things that Jasper allowed, but always he watched.

After his knives were unrolled and his stoves were well hot, Jasper asked for the meat. Big iced trays were brought before him by the strapping kitchen boys. The two of them were rough, lean and towheaded with ruddy faces. The cords of muscle that ran up their arms bulged as they lifted the heavy, ice-laden trays, and a hint of animal sweat touched their brows. The fish that they brought before Jasper still smelled of the ocean and the blood of the beef had not even finished darkening.

"And what else?" Jasper asked. "Is that all?"

More trays were brought before him, the contents of each slightly stranger than the last. The head of an elk hunted from the lord's forest, squirrels still twitching in their deaths from traps outside the lord's gates, the stringy flesh of a wolf, newts sliced lengthwise... Jasper looked over his meat and called "What else?" and "Is that all?" until a full dozen trays of the chilled dead were brought before him.

Jasper raised his hand; he had seen enough. The kitchen boys disappeared to their other tasks and Jasper settled his eyes on the meat. The present week had seen stewed monkey, reduced to organ meat and cooked long and slow over a quivering flame until it was so tender that just a touch from the lord's fork would burst it, spilling its juices over roasted potatoes. Then there had been nearly raw pig, rolled in salt and smoked for a time before being rubbed with lime and herbs from the lord's expansive gardens. Over a bed of oven-wilted greens the pork preened with brave flavors and the hint of bacon touched it with the decadent.

What, Jasper asked himself, could stand above those dishes?

He stared at the ice trays and wondered until slowly the dish came to him. He reached out and touched the nearest kitchen woman on her shoulder and she jumped at the contact.

"Help me," he said. The two of them extracted a side of beef from one of the trays and hung it from a hook in the back room adjoining the kitchen. Jasper asked for a large shallow bowl and placed it below the uncut carcass like an offering. With one of his knives—a long, thick silver piece with a wicked edge—he sliced open the creature and allowed its essence to pool beneath it. He carved into the beast and extracted cuts so lean and juicy that his mouth watered at the uncooked selections.

Back in the kitchen he oversaw the preparation of his meal. Without a word the staff, trained up since birth, had begun readying potential complements. He walked among them, gently touching on the shoulder those who he thought had best anticipated his needs: the stout older woman whose name was Martha had cut carrots so thin and uniform that he had to use them, and he touched her shoulder. Another woman, whose name escaped him, had cut long curlicues of beetroot that looked like broken hearts. He touched her as well.

The dish was coming along in his head. He chose a cooled beef stock, made fresh that day, and began working it into what his mind saw. He commanded that the cow's blood be spiked with a dash of vinegar to discourage clotting and on the stove he added spices to his slowly simmering broth: cloves to awaken the senses and allspice to keep them open, a little garlic for body and fresh chopped peppers to ward off complacency. He added his cuts of beef that he knew would become creamy and soft in the soup, the carrots so finely cut that they made him smile, and the broken hearts of beetroot so red and delicate that he could have wept over them. Hours slipped away as the soup grew bolder and richer.

Jasper called for the blood and added it very carefully. Even still a fat drop spilled onto the underside of his wrist. He watched it ride the tendon down toward the crook of his arm, leaving a bright trail against his pale skin. He licked his wrist clean.

The soup bloomed with the blood's addition. It was no longer just a soup, but a creation with a beating, bloody heart. Jasper had it plated immediately with a dollop of squid's ink in the dead center of the bowl. The darkness fanned outward like phantasmal fingers.

Alongside the soup he served black bread baked by the lord's own bakery and a creamy drink on shaved ice to cool the lord's palate. When it was finished, the dishes were taken off to the lord's table with strict instructions on what was to be served and at which times. The lord of the manor, Mr. Hugh Echo, was not finicky about his dinner service nor did he hold elaborate dinner parties but Jasper considered dinner a sacred affair and quietly encouraged the staff to do the same.

After dinner was served, Jasper dismissed much of the kitchen staff, but retained a few just in case the lord was displeased with dinner and wanted something else made. It had never happened before, but Jasper always wanted to be prepared. He had them clean, wash, and ready the unused portions of the dinner for donation to the kitchens of the town's poor in the morning.

Hours passed and Jasper finally relented and let the last of the kitchen staff go to their rooms. He knew where to find them if he needed them. He himself awaited the arrival of the butler, who always came to inform Jasper that the lord had retired. Before long he heard the heavy, familiar steps of the butler. The man, Rudolf Feathersport, entered the kitchen with a jacket in hand and spoke in his melodiously arch tone.

"The lord of the manor requests your presence in his solar," Rudolf said. "I surmised you would not have a jacket at the ready and so took the liberty of bringing you one."

"The lord wants to see me? Do you know what this regards?" Jasper asked.

Rudolf raised a manicured eyebrow. "Food, I presume."

Jasper put on the jacket and smoothed his hair back into a neater ponytail than usual. It wasn't the most decorous look, but it would have to do.

He followed Rudolf up through the bones of the manor. They took the back stairwells rather than going up the grand staircase at the front of the house. Through an incomprehensible zigzagging path they arrived before a mahogany door. Rudolf rapped twice with his knuckles, opened the door for Jasper and stepped aside. Jasper took a step into the room and then Rudolf, as if it had been prearranged, closed the door gently behind him.

Jasper glanced around the room quickly as not to seem like the moony-eyed son of some pauper gawking at the belongings of his betters. There was a painting of the late lord Herbert Echo, grandfather of the current lord, with a stern expression and a ceremonial black sash across his chest. He was tall and dark-featured, handsome in a steely way.

There were crests on the wall, a splendid oak desk and richly draped windows that were all attractive sights, but it was the carpet that drew Jasper's eye. Perhaps it was because his gaze was lowered, but the deep scarlet carpet stood out. It was like a cask of red wine had been breached and allowed to bleed.

"Mr. Jasper Roux, it is a genuine pleasure to finally make

your acquaintance," said Mr. Hugh Echo to his chef.

Jasper was quick with his courtesies. "I'm sure the pleasure is mine entirely, Mr. Echo."

"You must be wondering why I called you here so late at night."

"I'm certain you have your reasons, Mr. Echo."

"Please call me Hugh and there's no need for you to stare at the floor. I promise my gaze won't turn you to stone."

Jasper looked up. Hugh Echo was strongly built. He had long dark curls, olive skin and a neat mustache. Add to this his high boots and the close cut of his jacket, and he looked like nothing so much as a pirate captain from a story. His eyes were striking, dark mirrors for the burning candles throughout the solar. "There. Isn't that better?"

"Of course," Jasper responded. His own hair seemed ridiculous bordering upon comical in Hugh's company. His skin pallid and his posture limp. He straightened himself up, or tried.

Hugh gave him a strange look. "You remind me of someone, but I can't for the life of me remember.... Do you have any family that once worked at Echo Manor?"

"No, sir. Only myself."

"Ah, I see. I must be mistaken. Well, I won't worry you for a moment longer. The reason I called you here, Mr. Roux—"

"Jasper," the chef said. "If you insist that I call you Hugh, I mean. You might at least consider calling me Jasper."

The lord of the manor bent his head to indicate that a fair point had been made. "Jasper. I called you here not to chastise or worry you, but to give you my highest compliment. Your soup...blood soup was it?"

"Indeed, it was. A variation on a very old recipe."

"Yes. That blood soup was—you outdid yourself, my man.

The flavors were bursting with life and the presentation: sinister and romantic both. It was a delight. So much so that I almost disdained involving the bread, as fine as it was. And I almost turned away your cream refreshment so as not to spoil the taste; indeed, I let it linger on my tongue like..." Hugh smiled. "I fear simile would do the dish a disservice. Suffice to say that I enjoyed it very much."

"I am quite pleased to hear that..." Jasper said, adding, "...Hugh."

"I was so impressed that I had to meet the man behind the creation and ask him a favor."

"A favor?"

Hugh brought his hands together and raised them over his mouth as if in deep concentration or prayer. His brows furrowed. He brought his hands back down again, knitting them in front of him, but the crease in his brow remained.

"I confess that I still have a taste for something novel," Hugh said.

"That's no favor at all. I'll have the kitchen staff awoken at once—"

"That won't be necessary," Hugh said, then asked, "How long have you worked here, Jasper?"

"Eight years."

"Eight years. How old were you when you started here?"

Jasper paused to think about it. "Roughly twenty six?"

"And in eight years' time, what rumors have you heard about me?"

Jasper flinched. "Pardon me?"

Hugh strode across the dark-red carpet, the sound of his footfalls lost in the sumptuous fibers. He reached up with his long arms and fingered the Echo crest high on the wall.

"Rumors, gossip, hearsay. You must have heard something, even if you don't do much fraternizing. It's hard to keep your ears closed for eight years, Jasper."

Hugh turned back to Jasper. The reflection of the candle flames gave his eyes a hellish glow.

"What have you heard about why I don't leave this manor? Why I keep it empty unlike my grandfather, who so loved parties and galas and fêtes? Who could not wake happily in the morning but for the sound of his children shouting his name." Hugh grinned and moved away from the crest. His attention fell solely on Jasper once again. "Tell me what you've heard."

"Hugh—"

"It's all right. Just say it."

Jasper sighed. "They say it makes you sick to leave the grounds, that you have fits, tremors. I suppose I've heard that it grows worse in public, when you're around people, so you keep the manor empty," Jasper said, clutching his hands behind his back.

"In my grandfather's final years he must have thought me a disappointment. Two sons lost to war, a sister to illness, and my mother as well. His only surviving grandson a shut-in, a cripple. I doubt we shared much beside a name. I wasn't even here when he died. I hardly knew him." Hugh stroked his chin. "But we both loved food, I do know that. His chef was one of the best in the world, brought here through great personal cost to my grandfather and lavished with gifts. He served here for twelve years and for each of those twelve he was given a knife, a knife unlike any in the world. That was before the war, before things changed. Alas."

Hugh shook his head as if memories could be as water flying off of a dog's back.

"But let's discuss why I brought you here. What I want from you," Hugh said, again walking across the room. "As you can see I am not a sickly man. The rumors are only half right on that account. I do disdain crowds, but that is because of what I am. There is no word to accurately describe it because I think I am the only one that there has ever been. I spent my years abroad searching for someone, anyone who could do what I can. As the years passed it grew worse, more powerful and I grew frail in the company of others. All that time and all that pain...I found nothing. I found no one."

"And what is it that you can do?" Jasper asked.

"I can see...I can sense..." Hugh made a frustrated noise. "I can taste what others have tasted, see what others have seen, feel what they've felt. I can see that you don't believe me. Perhaps you think this is too incredible to be true and why would I blame you? I wish it were a lark."

"How?" Jasper said; it was all he could say.

Hugh came toward him directly and touched a finger to his lips. Jasper recoiled, surprised. Then Hugh took that same finger and put it to his own mouth. Hugh's tongue, pink and wet, licked the tip of his finger. He closed his eyes.

"Blood. I taste blood."

"The cow's blood, a drop I licked up earlier. Forgive me, Hugh, but I made you blood soup. It's hardly surprising you would think of blood. Hardly miraculous," Jasper responded calmly.

Hugh opened his eyes. They were sleepy and far-off, still in the midst of whatever reverie had come over him.

"You're...you're right. That was silly of me, I suppose. Here: give me your hand."

Jasper presented his right hand and Hugh raised both of his.

Hugh's fingers traced over Jasper's fingers, feeling every callus and every ridge. His fingers slid up to Jasper's palm and over the smoother skin on the alternate side. Their thumbs touched and Hugh pressed his into Jasper's as if there were something there to find, some secret just beneath the skin.

"A bone handle. A stained oak grip. A thick iron knife with a sharper edge than most. A man's throat…"

Jasper ripped his hand away at that and Hugh blinked hard, squinting and groaning softly as if the candlelight were too much.

"I'm…sorry, Mr. Echo. I'm not sure I'm comfortable…"

"No, no. I should apologize. I didn't mean to look so deeply. I didn't realize what I would find."

"If it's all the same to you, Mr. Echo, I'd like to go—"

"No!" Hugh shouted. There was an edge of panic in his voice, but he tried admirably to smooth it out. "I mean, let me apologize. Again, I didn't mean to pry. Your personal business is your own. Can we start again?"

"What do you want from me?" Jasper whispered. His eyes again on the bloody carpet.

"I want to taste the most wonderful flavor you've ever encountered. You've trained all over the world. I can barely leave this room anymore. Let me taste the flavor you've enjoyed most in your travels. That's all I ask of you. Then, if you wish to leave my employ you may do so with a stipend twice what I pay you now. I ask only that you keep my secret."

Jasper looked up at his employer whose expression was suddenly frail, and asked, "How?"

"Think on the flavor: the taste of it, the texture of it. Close your eyes. I'll do the rest," Hugh explained.

Jasper hesitated, but he did as he was asked. He closed his

eyes and thought of a pastry he'd once tried. It was flaky and warm. It was buttery and seemed to melt on his tongue. The inside was hot and sticky with jam. It was sweet and tart at the same time.

He was thinking of this when Hugh's lips touched his and Hugh's tongue slipped into his partially opened mouth. Then he was no longer thinking of pastries.

He thought of a man whose tongue had tasted of jam and whose fingers had been nimble—how they were warm and how they'd left him sticky. It had been a long time ago, a lifetime perhaps or longer, but that touch still lingered.

He thought of a tongue on his, sweet and tart at the same time. He thought of a body that had been hot against his. How the two of them had struggled in crimson sheets and sweat until the sanguine sheets turned black against their skin.

He thought of a man's neck, his thighs, his dark hair and olive skin, his arms corded thickly with muscle. A tall man with dark features and iron in his gaze. A man whose hands were always slightly cool in the beginning and then hot by the end. A man whose hungers were prodigious.

He thought of this other man's tongue in his mouth among other things. He thought of this man's desire expanding and bursting under his touch. The hushed groans and mouths clamped tight to keep noises from spilling out into the night, up through the floorboards of the old house, out amongst the trees hemming in the verdant garden. He thought of everywhere their bodies had been. And the variety of fluids that had passed between them, each containing a promise or a provocation or an incitement to further debauchery.

He thought of this man's sweet, tart meat.

Jasper pulled away and Hugh's eyes fluttered open sleepily.

It took the head of the household a moment to regain himself and another long moment before he lowered his own gaze to where Jasper's stare had fixated below his waist. Not only was Hugh fully erect, but fluid was dripping through his trousers.

Jasper tried to spare the man further embarrassment by raising his eyes, but he could not unsee the pulsing outline of Hugh's manhood or the slick trail it left on his trousers. The unmistakable smell of semen permeated the space between the two men. Hugh drew his jacket closed, but it did not entirely hide what was now staining the inner thigh of his cream-colored trousers.

"I'm...I can't," Hugh said. "I didn't expect that. There were so many things I saw. Tasted. I'm not sure..."

"Will that be all for the evening, Mr. Echo?" Jasper asked. He licked his lips and cleared his throat as if a powerful thirst had come upon him.

"Wait, Jasper. Just wait a moment. I don't want you to go yet."

"In a few hours the sun will be up and with it, your daytime chef. If there's anything I can have him prepare for you, I can leave a note."

"You're not like me, but you're not like anyone else. Are you?" Hugh asked.

Jasper met his gaze. "I'm a chef. And I'm loyal to this family. I will be back tomorrow night and the night after that if you'll still have me. But right now I have to go."

Hugh nodded, and Jasper turned to leave.

"Was my grandfather a good man? A kind man?" Hugh asked suddenly.

"I'm sure he was," Jasper said. "I'm not the right person to ask."

"Yes, you're right. If you had known him that would make you very old, wouldn't it? Improbably so..."

"May I see myself out?"

Hugh hesitated, but in the end he smiled and answered politely. "Of course. Thank you, chef, for your service."

The chef gave a courteous nod and then left the room. He found his way back through the manor and into the kitchen. He saw to it that everything was exactly as the daytime chef had left it. Once he was satisfied, Jasper went to the weathered wooden counter upon which generations of meals had been cooked. He stood before his leather pack and ran his fingers over each of his twelve knives before putting each one into its respective place. He rolled the pack up and bound it twice with a black cotton sash so well used that it was no longer, strictly speaking, black. At the sash's center had been an embroidered crest, but years had pulled the threads loose and the crest no longer identified any family or allegiance. Jasper ran his fingers over where the symbol had been before tucking the leather pack under his arm.

The chef left Echo Manor just as the sun was beginning to consider peeking up over the horizon. He would be gone by the time the first rays touched the ground. He always was.

THE ALCHEMIST'S DAUGHTER

Rosalía Zizzo

S o what are you working on now, Father?" While suppressing
my cough and the urge to chuckle at his wild hair, I toss
my own honey-blonde tresses over the shoulder of my sweaty
peasant blouse and then rub my father's back as I stand over
him. His rumpled wool shirt is covered in splatters from his
sloppy stirring, but I watch him mix yet another of his many
delicious concoctions in a stone jar anyway. I'm sarcastic, of
course. "Smashed beetles mixed with the juice from mushed
cherries?" I wish it were a joke. I really do.

My father looks like he hasn't slept in days, and he probably
hasn't. He's too preoccupied with mixing his elaborate fare.
He's wearing what looks like a burlap sack, and his unkempt,
shoulder-length hair is a mess, the greasy strands facing this
way and that, some even sticking straight up, with a couple of
gray patches visible from the mass of unwashed and disheveled
locks. The unshaven frizzy beard has grown below his chin,
and he looks like a joke of a man mixing a joke of a meal. But
he hasn't always been like this. Before my mother got sick, he

was known for his brilliance, and I'm sure his genius will shine again someday. Keyword: someday.

Perking up, he turns to me before resuming his work, and the look I see in his glazed, sea-green eyes is almost manic.

"I think I have it this time," he says excitedly while he stirs in a furious fashion, slopping his mixture everywhere. "I really think this time it's different."

Poor Father. He really lost it when Mother died. Usually he brings out his trusty mortar and pestle and grinds up seeds or berries in order to mix them with some foul-tasting liquid for me to drink, spilling the berries on my white frock. He's tenacious, and since I started exhibiting symptoms of the same illness my mother had before her death, he has been undying in his search for a way to save me—a cure, so to speak.

"Do you need help?" I grab his wrists to stop his frantic stirring and force his hands to the desk. We use our dining table as a desk, and he has turned the dining room/kitchen into his lab. I stare into his tired eyes. "I think it's time to rest, now."

I'm sure I don't look much better than he does with the dark circles under my sunken gray eyes that look bruised from lack of sleep and my bony frame that reveals my daily feast of whatever I can get my hands on, such as crumbs from our neighbors' bread and the meat from dead birds and rodents in combination with my father's beverages. My oily hair shows I haven't washed it for quite some time, and the smudges on my face and clothing prove my lack of desire to deal with bathing or the laundry. It's not like I have more than two dresses anyway, but I'm sure I look like my mother did in her last days.

The chronic cough is the first symptom, as well as the sickly, gaunt appearance and bloodshot eyes. Before the pallid, dry skin and the weight loss comes the ever-persistent cough, as if you're trying to rid your throat of a speck of dust that seems to linger no matter how hard you cough to expel it. My mother was always coughing, and she lost a lot of weight a couple of years ago, and her constant complaint about her sore throat and her persistent nausea made us seek out every doctor we could until we didn't have an ounce of gold left to afford to even feed ourselves. And then she died, bringing a host of religious followers, insisting she could have been saved if only she worshipped their invisible god. As if their god cared about their dreary music and bland food—and their hard, uncomfortable seating. Sounds like a god who doesn't know anything about having a good time.

When he starts experimenting with metals in his lab, I see the desperation in his eyes, the haggard and sallow expression on his face, and the dark grime under his fingernails. The solution to my ailment seems to elude him even though he attempts mixing all sorts of concoctions with the hope of eliminating my pain and anguish. All of the local New England population has even nicknamed him the village lunatic, stomping past our doorway and throwing rotten fruit while laughing hysterically. And some even claim he is in league with the devil, accusing him of absurd activities while insisting he has committed absolutely outrageous acts like dancing in the moonlight naked or flying over the rooftops every misty evening.

"Come here, my dear," my hardworking father says while reaching toward me and grasping my filthy apron, pulling me closer so that I scrape the bottoms of my shoes on the wooden floor. As he drags me, I inch along in my slightly heeled shoes with buckles on top the size of my index finger, and I hope I don't leave more mud on the floor. The grimy, tan-colored shoes have mud splattered all over them, attesting to the muddy streets outside.

"Everybody wants to make their own gold. I'm just different in that I also hope to ease your pain." I nod with the hope of looking encouraging, but it doesn't seem to help.

After running his hand vigorously back and forth over his head, further mussing his hair, he groans, "I refuse to have you live through Matilde's misery." He sighs loudly and cries out my name. "Elizabeth! What am I to do, Elizabeth?" Looking to be at his wit's end, he focuses his eyes on me and lifts his eyebrows.

"It's all right, Father. I'm just tired is all. Perhaps I just need some more sleep." I try to soothe him with my voice and my touch, but any attempt to take him away from his task at hand is completely ineffectual. He ignores anything I do or say, and when another string of coughs erupts from my mouth, he pounds the table and sets his elbows on the wood before burying his face in his palms. I'm sure his groaning can be heard from the next town.

Feeling helpless about his mental anguish, all I can do is massage his shoulders and run my hands over his arms until I hear a crowd moving closer to our door. I turn my head and walk over. When I crack the door open and peer outside, I stop breathing. I notice the most beautiful man I've ever seen in my life with a giant cross around his neck blinking his long lashes over liquid, dark eyes in front of a noisy mass of people, waving whatever tools they have collected.

"What are you doing?" I shout, trying to keep my voice from breaking as the man holds his arm in full swing, ready to hurl an overripe piece of fruit at my front door. "Why don't you leave us alone?" Tempted to throw garbage back at him,

I rush outside and grab his arm, tackling him to the ground, which is the only thing stopping the mob behind him from murdering my father with their pitchforks and kitchen knives. They tumble over us in their effort to get to the door, but they only end up making a muddy pile of silly fools. Panic and mass hysteria seemed to follow after my mother passed away, and the crowd mobilized outside our door. Too bad this particular fellow has joined them, so his good looks are wasted.

Any follower of the mob lacks the brainpower necessary to be considered a worthy man, and eating the fruit would be a better idea than throwing it. At least, that's what I think.

"I, um, am only..." Dropping the purple fruit when he falls with me on top of him, he tries to compose himself as his three-cornered hat falls into the mud, and in his embarrassment, he fumbles over himself as he struggles to stand, apologizing profusely. But that doesn't change my opinion of him: I see him as willing to murder someone because the crowd thinks it's a good idea, a fool who deserves a slap to make his sly smile disappear.

"Go. Away."

When I go back inside, my father questions me.

"Anyone we know?"

"No, Father. It's just those demented people saying stupid things." *As well as the most handsome man in the world.*

Slamming my journal shut in the evening and capping the fountain pen, I ponder my options as I place the book and pen on my makeshift nightstand, an old dusty crate that has worn, faded crimson paint on the back. I settle in for the night, but my stomach growls again as I attempt sleep, and I can't help but think of the wonderful foods my mother and I used to make together.

We used to create some amazing holiday fare and some scrumptious desserts I loved to share with our friends and neighbors when we joined them in merrymaking. That was when they didn't treat us like outcasts and when they invited us to gatherings, but I guess we don't deserve their friendship anymore because, according to them, we only party with the devil now— as if that's more believable than grieving over a dead spouse or worrying about whether or not you will suffer the same fate as your mother. Entertaining the red-skinned demon is a more acceptable reason for not sleeping according to them.

In order to get any sleep at all, I stroke myself to a fantasy of the dark-eyed stranger, the man leading the mob of angry lunatics carrying kitchen utensils and garden implements. Not his behavior, but his smile and his eyes. And the feel of his strong arms pinning me to the bed. My mattress probably isn't the softest, but it's my own. Like my mind. Like my fantasy of a man I'd like to touch, whose firm chest calls to my lips and hands. His strong thighs and muscular arms serve as relief from the pain of losing my mother, the anguish from watching my father change from a brilliant to a crazed man, and my extraordinary hunger.

In the morning, I humble myself, lift my skirts so they don't get muddy, and walk toward the marketplace beside the Jefferson farm. My father needs food, and I remember when my mother was still alive I would accompany her to the marketplace to sell our eggs from our chickens. Over time, we eventually ate all the eggs and then the chickens as well. The mud created by last night's drizzle splatters on my ankles, but I know that if I don't find a way for the two of us to get some food, we'll starve. As it is, my father is already behaving like a demented person with his lack of food and sleep, and his concern for me has turned him into a mad recluse.

Slowly approaching the table with Mister Jefferson fussing over local produce and jars of jam, I straighten my dress and rub my lips together, pinch my cheeks, and comb my fingers through my hair. Mister Jefferson looks up and addresses me.

"Why, Elizabeth! I haven't seen you in a while. I was going to talk to you at church, but you haven't been there for quite some time. I heard about your mother. I am so so sorry..." His eyes look warm and sincere, even though I can tell his mind is elsewhere. Regardless, I take a deep breath and say what I planned to say.

"I would like to talk to you, sir—" Distracted, he turns and yells over his shoulder.

"Samuel!" Turning back to me, he reassures me, "I'm sorry. I have to go. It's all right. You're in good hands with my nephew who's come to stay with us. Now I need to help Sarah with the maple syrup made from the sap tapped from the Adams's trees."

Before I can respond, he's already gone, and his nephew has taken his place. The nephew is clean and presentable and completely like a businessman marketing his wares, but when I look at his face, I gasp.

"You!" I see his deep brown eyes that make me melt like a puddle of churned butter left out in the midday sun. So his nephew's name is Samuel. Now his strong farmworker's build makes sense. Lifting heavy equipment must make for his huge biceps, or maybe it's from chopping wood or from hoisting huge sacks of flour over his shoulder. Regardless, it's going to take a lot more than a desirable body to change my mind about him. I briefly scan his chest and shoulders while I collect my thoughts. At least I can fantasize about him. It doesn't mean I have to like him.

"Elizabeth?" He questions me with that smirk that makes me feel like I just swallowed a boulder. I quickly close my knees.

"Yyyes..." My mind is swimming with many thoughts, some of them hateful and some of them lustful, but I finally spit it out. "Well, I came here to see if there was anything I could do to earn some food to fill my father's stomach. He needs to eat." It feels like the temperature has risen a couple of degrees higher when I look into his eyes.

"Of course. I will make up a package you can take with you." His grin crinkles the sides of his eyes, and the spreading pink flush over his cheeks makes him even more handsome if that's at all possible.

I didn't plan on begging for charity. "I can work for it. I just don't have any money to pay you right now." I scowl and then tentatively lower my eyes, looking at him through the veil of my eyelashes so I don't have to look into his eyes directly. My heart pounds.

"That's all right. I will give you something to take with you, Elizabeth. I'm honestly embarrassed about the other day. My mates dared me to—" He pauses as he begins collecting things for my father. "I'm sorry about your mother." His eyes look down at his hands that are gathering items for me. "I'm sorry about the other day." His apology seems lost in the growing sexual tension. Samuel wraps the items in paper and ties a long-sleeved shirt around the load, pushing them toward me, but my pride prevents me from snatching the items immediately. Instead, I offer more explanation so that I don't accept an excuse for his rotten behavior so easily.

"I don't want you to take pity on me. I am just frightened for my father."

"Of course." I hear sarcasm in his voice, but that's probably because I've already prejudged him. After I freeze, tears begin to form as I think about my father and about a possible new plan. What was I thinking coming here? The cussed fool doesn't deserve any more of my time.

"Forget it." I feel stupid now. I quickly turn and head back in the direction I came, but just as I take a step, he reaches out and seizes my clothing.

"Wait, wait, wait. I had no intention of offending you. I promise to help. Really. I promise." His sparkling eyes look sincere, and he grabs hold of the load. "Here. Let me accompany you." He starts to follow me, but I stop him.

"No, no, no. That's not necessary, but I don't think my father's strong enough to—"

"I understand." When he sees me pinch my brows together in skepticism, he reassures me: "Really." We meet each other's eyes and gaze for a moment, him blinking his long lashes until he inhales sharply and adjusts his breeches.

"He's mixing all sorts of things together and having me drink them. He worries about me." I chatter on and on, and when Samuel sees my continued difficulty, he steps forward, lowering his voice as he bends down near my ear.

"Really. It's all right. I understand. We'll take care of your food." His warm breath on my ear makes me sizzle. He pushes the items back toward me slightly and gestures with his head that I should take them.

I reach toward the package, but my hands hover over it as I lift my eyes to meet his, where I see heat within the dark chocolate irises. He wiggles and adjusts his trousers again as we stare at each other for quite some time.

When I finally see that he is sincere, I hesitantly grab the items to head back home, not caring if my petticoats will get mud on them. "Thank you," I mutter.

As I scoop up my belongings and quickly march home, Abigail, my shadow for the past ten years, appears and trots by my side.

"Hi, Elizabeth! Did you hear?" She always sounds out of breath and excited. She scurries along at my side like a four-year-old as I speed along.

"Hi, Abigail." My monotone voice sounds cold and restrained and hopefully slows her childish skipping. "Hear what?"

Panting audibly, she tries to keep up with my pace. "They accused a girl in the next town over of working with Lucifer." She takes a deep breath. "They're going to burn her next week!" I stop briefly in front of our shed-like home and stare at her, cradling the food in front of me and losing myself in thought as she continues her story.

"Burn?" I feel numb while I turn to the door and climb the steps, not hearing anything further Abigail says because the world has become a confusing and lonely place.

When I walk through the front door, my father is still working, mixing something in a stone bowl. He looks up and asks, "Where have you been? You should see what I've been working on. I think this one will work." His eyes glitter in excitement, but I refrain from joining him in his joy. I put on a face of seriousness and grab his hands to stop his stirring, gazing into his eyes. "I've been working on it all day and—"

"I was at the Jefferson farm." I push the wrapped items toward him. "Eat something now."

"You should see if this helps!" He yanks his hands away and resumes his stirring, each rotation with the spoon causing another outburst. "It might." He circles around once.

"Help you." He circles around again. "It might work!" In his excitement, he gets even sloppier.

"All right. After you get something to eat."

He stares at me while holding the bowl in front of him. Seconds tick by, and when I don't take the bowl from him but instead nod toward the pile on the table, he stops and looks at it, and when his mind processes what I've just said, he gradually stops speaking altogether. "They gave you food?" His eyes fix on what I brought, and his lips go slack for a while.

After staring at the shirt tied around the food, he looks back at me and then wavers between my stoic face and the lump in front of him. Seconds tick by with him looking back and forth between my face and the pile in front of him until he reaches both hands out and snatches the parcel in a flash, going for the knots, ripping open the sleeves around the whole bundle.

When he successfully unveils the ingredients of the load, he tosses the paper aside and reveals a glass jar filled with something red, a loaf of bread, apples, carrots, celery and beets. When he paws through everything, two small pieces of maple candy tumble out, and he very un-gracefully pops one into his mouth before he follows it with wolfing down item after item, chewing with his mouth open until he looks up at me and asks me to join him.

"Did you eat already, Elizabeth? Here. Have something." He doesn't even wait for me to shake my head *no* before he tears the loaf of bread in half and devours one piece, swallowing as quickly as possible while tossing me the other half. He even opens the jar of jam and shoves his fingers inside the jar, scooping out the jam and licking it from his fingers, the jam dripping from his hand and beard.

It feels good to see my father get something in his belly, and it feels satisfying to have something in mine as well. For the time being, I don't feel like my gut is turning inside out. He may not be a gentleman, and I may not be a lady right now, but at least my father and I can think about something other than searching for a meal, and have a night where we can actually sleep. My father, not to be deterred, returns his attention to his strange soup.

"Now drink this," he says, his mouth dripping with jam as he holds the bowl in front of me again.

I had hoped he had forgotten, but I made my father a deal, so I appease him by swallowing the entire contents of the bowl in one gulp. It's warm and acidic and makes me wish for one of my mother's homemade tasty treats.

The following day I walk out the door and immediately shield my eyes with my hand as I squint and head toward the Jefferson farm again where I meet up with Samuel—who looks as good as ever. His rich brown eyes complement his wavy dark hair that, I'm grateful to see, hasn't been covered with a wig or tied into a ponytail, but instead flows down to the top of his black waistcoat with a frilly shirt beneath it, and the sight ignites a small flame in my gut. I lower my eyes and share my gratitude for his generosity.

"Thank you for yesterday. It was good to see my father eat." I pause. "Well, that's not completely true. His table manners were atrocious, but it was good to know his stomach was full so he could work more on his experiments."

"I'm glad." His smile destroys any negativity I feel at the moment, and his dark eyes look liquid as he gazes at me, while his waistcoat twists when he turns to fuss over the vegetables, showing off his muscular forearms. I could only imagine what he would look like stripped of all his clothing. While gazing at him, I get the sudden urge to speak.

"So, um…" He jerks his head toward me, and I feel the flush spreading in my cheeks as I inhale. "That's it. Thank you." I prepare to bolt.

"Of course." He smiles just enough to heat my insides. "I hope you come back when you need to." If I weren't afraid of being burned alive by the mob, I would invite him over before leaving. "And I hope you got some food as well." I nod my head once as he passes me a broken bit of cheese, accidentally brushing his fingers against my hand, which sends a charge through my arm as I take off. Perhaps there's more to him than what I had originally thought.

As I go through my day, I notice a few things about my body that haven't always been there. For one, my reaction time is quite a bit faster. And my eyes seem a little more sensitive to sunlight. After a bit, I notice my coughing looks to have disappeared as well. My imagination? Perhaps, but I don't know.

After several days, I see Samuel when I head into town. He walks on the same side of the street coming toward me, and the closer he gets the hotter I feel. I haven't been able to stop thinking about him: his eyes and smile, his arms, his body underneath his clothing as well as his true personality—and about what was going through his mind when he came to our door prepared to throw that rotting piece of fruit.

My heart pounds as I do my best to avoid his gaze. The nearer he is to me the more nervous I become until he acknowledges me with a tilt of his hat and says, "Good day." And then he stops himself midstride. "You are quite um, um…" I quicken my pace, preparing for him to finish his sentence. Tall? Pale?

"...Beautiful," he says with a soft voice as I pass by. Quickly turning my head behind me, I pause, speechless. He thinks I'm beautiful? We gaze into each other's eyes as we stand in the street until we hear Mister Jefferson shout.

"Samuel!"

We break away suddenly, and I continue walking very slowly as he sprints away. Taking step after gradual step, I think about what he just said. Beautiful? My mother is the only one who has ever called me beautiful. This is the first day I have ever received such a compliment from someone other than her. It's also the day I start hearing whispers whenever I come within range of other people in town.

"She has the same sickness as her mother."

"Witchcraft..."

"I saw her talking with Sam Jefferson..."

Whenever I walk into town, someone says something about my father that is completely untrue, like he's been drinking a potion made with bird feathers so he can fly or creating a pile of gold coins by mixing together dead animals and his own blood. And the things they say about me? Well, if I weren't so worried about my father's life and my own future, I would laugh at them all. It gets so I'm terrified of being around anyone though, including Samuel, especially Samuel: the man I fantasize about at night, who occupies my thoughts every day.

One day, the sun shines brightly in the sky, and I see Samuel in town across the street as I shade my eyes with my hand while I walk toward the school. His three-cornered hat appears weathered, but his white linen shirt looks clean and fits perfectly over his broad shoulders as he moves, swinging his arms with each stride. Why he creates such a visceral response in me is confusing, and I run my index finger under my nose to wipe the sweat that has accumulated there as I march along.

When I notice him occasionally looking up, I increase my speed and face the other way, hoping to avoid his glance, but he happens to look up just when I increase speed, and he runs across the street in his breeches that fit securely just below the knees and then makes huge strides toward me.

The hint of a smirk and his wolfish leer merely darken his eyes, and just when he is within reach, he catches my arm and pulls me to him so that I cry out and stare wide-eyed into his eyes from an inch away. His touch makes my heart pound so loud I can hear it in my ears, and I can feel his breath on my face when he speaks to me.

"Come with me," he says as he yanks me toward his uncle's farm, and as we stumble over the ground, I think that this is it: the last day I will ever see the sun shining in the sky. The end.

As I try to pull away from his grasp, I shout for him to stop. "No! Don't hurt me!" I try not to make a scene, muffling my voice as much as I can so others don't hear, and I attempt to keep the panic out of my voice when I ask, "Is it true? Are the things I hear true?" He gives me a confused look as he pulls me into the barn. "Is your family responsible for spreading the lies and the nonsense about my father being in league with the devil?" I scan the area for an exit. "Are you going to burn me alive?" He comes to a grinding halt and looks into my face, like I have just hit him across the jaw with a cast-iron skillet.

"What?"

My whole body feels numb, my lips tingle and my heart hammers in my chest. "Please. Please, don't hurt me." I shiver as I once again look for an exit.

"Sh, sh, sh…" He holds my hand firmly and looks in my eyes while waiting for my panic to dissipate. "Elizabeth, my lady fair, calm down. My aunt and uncle might have old beliefs and strange ideas, and I feel embarrassed about falling prey to such ideas a couple weeks ago, but I have no intention of harming you. You have more chance of lighting me on fire because of your stormy eyes and milky-white skin. Really. Your beauty sets me aflame." He holds me firmly to his chest, and I stop struggling to ponder what he's just said. "It's all right now. Sh..." He kisses each cheek while waiting for my eyes to meet his.

Letting the information sink in, I try to relax as he embraces me, but the calm I feel from relief is short-lived as he presses his lips against mine and threads his fingers through my hair, cupping my head in his hands and kissing my neck, which leaves me completely breathless. *Beautiful. He thinks I'm beautiful.* My lips continue to quiver as he soothes me by stroking my hair and shushing me while he captures my arms and sets me away from him so I can continue to stare into his eyes. His smirk stops me for the time being.

"All right?" he asks while I nod, which is really to convince myself the terror has disappeared while he runs a palm down my arm and grabs my hand, raising the back of it to his lips, giving it a little kiss and lingering for just a moment before dropping it but not letting go. Giving my hand a little tug then, he moves me forward while guiding me into a stall.

"I...I...I..."

"It's all right, milady." He stops and presses his mouth to the dip in my neck below my ear where my heart pulses, and every second he remains there makes my heart pound harder, my knees weaken, and my lower region tingle. Time seems to stand still. I swallow hard, looking into Samuel's face when he raises it from my throat.

"Do you—?"

"Sh…" A tiny droplet has spilled from my eye, and he kisses it away and then pets my hair and kisses each temple with his wet lips. "It's going to be all right." As I give in to his gentle stroking, I nod, and he lightly nibbles my lower lip until I stop shaking. It takes some time.

Then the arousal really begins. I am aware of his lips on my body and of his warm hands moving slowly down my head. His attention feels amazing, and my acceptance of it comes easily once I give myself permission to believe he actually finds me beautiful.

The pace of my breathing changes as well as the beat of my heart for a different reason other than fear now, but I can't seem to take a full breath. Every kiss sears my skin, and every kiss adds to the flame flickering in my gut. He presses his lips to my cheek and then presses light kisses down my throat to the top of my bosom rising above my corset and at risk of spilling from the top of my dress. And then when he gets to the soft fleshy hills, I pant even more shallowly than I have been.

My fantasy has come to life, and I'm burning up. I feel like I sometimes do when I'm sick and the heat of my face creates a sweaty film on my upper lip. My heart hammers in my chest. I'm dizzy and flushed and unsure as to whether or not this is my illness creeping up on me or my deep desire to have Samuel's weight atop my body. I crave the power. I want his masculinity.

Samuel pushes me gently but forcefully into a corner before reaching to tug on the cord at my throat, untying the bow, and I feel the slickness as if I've wet my finger with my spittle and am about to stroke myself like I do at night. Slowly walking me backward toward a bale of hay, he quickly removes his waistcoat and lays it out, then lifts me and sets me down on top of it, looking me in the eyes. The heat there is unmistakable, and at this point I'm willing to give him anything.

Fixing his eyes on me and inhaling deeply through his nose, he grabs my ankles, turning me so I'm lying face up. Then he raises my skirts and spreads my legs, groaning as he steps between them. We say the words, "I want you," simultaneously because as much as it feels like the world is crumbling around us, we are drawn to each other and can't deny it. For whatever reason, we need each other. I wipe the sweat from above my upper lip and watch as Samuel unbuttons his trousers.

"My blood boils for you, Elizabeth," he tells me as he lowers his britches to his thighs and wraps his fist around his cock, pulling it up and down. I hold my breath and let the air out gradually as he drags both sets of fingers from my knees to my thighs, where he squeezes handfuls of flesh while gazing at me like he's in a trance.

Parting my lips, I watch him stroke himself unconsciously as he takes a step. In silence, he looks me over and very, very slowly runs his tongue along his lips while inching closer. Moving farther between my legs, he places the head of his cock at the entrance while he circles my waist with his hands and pushes forward, slipping the fat head into me.

"Oh!" I can't tell if the noise is coming from me or him.

His sinking into me stops me from voicing any actual words. The noises are more grunts and sounds than anything intelligible. Thrust after thrust increases the pace of my breathing, and my heart is beating so hard I fear it will burst soon. I can't sit still. My legs move up and down involuntarily, and each time he comes away from my body, I arch my back so that I lift myself up to meet him. I want him to crush me beneath him. I want to feel his heat above me. I want his moist clothing and skin and damp hair along his scalp to announce our passion to the world.

He pumps until I hold my breath and tense my legs, and he thrusts one last time and my orgasm erupts like an explosion from a red-hot ember, spitting fire throughout my entire body—all the way to my chest and up to my ears. My body racks with him inside me, and soon after I feel him tense before he shoots jets of hot liquid again and again, his weight now atop me, the pleasure slowly dissipating and my heartbeat and breathing returning to normal.

Time stands still, and I want to stay locked in his arms forever because worries don't exist there. Not a one. No worry about my attractiveness, no worry that I will forever be alone, no fear of being burned alive, and no disease. We stay wrapped around each other for quite some time, but after a bit, I decide to inform him about my ailment. Strange timing, but I have no idea when to bring it up. "You know I'm sick, right?" We stay locked together in silence, and I hold my breath before he responds.

"Yes, milady." I can barely hear him, and his voice lacks emotion.

"And you know there is no cure, right?" The silence is almost deafening.

"Yes, I know." He doesn't say anything further, and since I don't know what else to do, I fix my clothing and go home, my feelings a jumbled mess of longing and uncertainty.

When I return home, my father, who has been waiting for me, looks me over from head to toe while holding another cup.

"Elizabeth. What happened? You look…"

"I, um, think I love him…"

"Who?"

* * *

As I finish reading to my companion, I set the diary down.

"In the morning, the sunshine hurt my eyes so badly I stumbled toward the wardrobe, where I climbed in and curled up all day." I look into his eyes. "Many people believe vampirism started in Europe, but we know the truth: it all started as a side effect from one of my father's concoctions that had combined with my disease, at the dawn of chemistry as a science, about half a century after the witch hunt trials started in Salem. I discovered my need for blood soon after. Without it, as you know, the disease returns; with it, we are immune to every disease, including the ultimate disease of death.

"Apparently, it can be passed on through saliva, blood or tears, so we choose our lovers very carefully now in the twenty-first century. Isn't that right, Samuel?"

The Hollow in the Black Cliffs

Madeleine Swann

rozen waves crash against dark rocks and wind slices through the grassland. The villagers hardly notice the sea air blowing salt and brine through their brick houses anymore—they, their cart horses and sheep are the sturdiest in the land. My lithe body and long hair, both black as midnight, are buffeted in the wind and I cover myself with my wings for warmth. I grip with hands and toes on to the branches of a tree and watch the men scamper through the mist like plague rats over their fishing boats, nothing but wood and ropes to protect them from the giant squid and her kind. Their wives collect fresh water from the well, telling tales and tittering as it spills from buckets down their long skirts. Their hair is covered by cloth caps and their eyes gleam with scandal.

The men are laughing raucously, red hands tying rigging and nets. My grip tightens around my own piece of netting, stolen from one of their ships several moons ago. A stout, white-bearded man is the first coherent voice I can hear. "She'll be out on the rob in a day or two, mark my words."

"You can't know that, Sam Rudden," scoffs another as he pulls at ropes with calloused fingers.

"I know it well enough," is the reply. "Predictable as the seasons is our lady of the sky, the Black Widow. And mark you this, young Eli will be her target." He gestures to a dark-haired man more slender and delicate than the others. His eyes flick nervously over his tasks and his hands are not as certain. He laughs at the mention of his name and looks down at his feet.

"Eli?" scoffs one of the burlier types.

"Aye," says the old man. "I've been living a good many years, Markus. I know better than most her pattern. They say she's one of the last of her kind, ain't none of her own left to fertilize her eggs. Those things that hatch though—weird twisted creatures neither one nor the other. Yet still she tries."

"Well, let's hope she waits till after tomorrow."

There is a hint of bitterness in the old man's voice. I am furious too; the suggestion of my predictability is an insult. I don't follow the eternal, dreary patterns year after year, season after season like man. I purse my lips indignantly, though in honesty his words sting because they're true. I have chosen Eli. He has pianist's fingers and a dreamer's blue eyes; he should be painting in Italy, not slaving by a cliff side. I notice his gaze flit like a moth to something nearby.

I strain my neck to see what he sees. She's standing at the edge of the grassland, before the ground turns to sand. She's kneeling beside a little boy and gesturing to the boat. He's a toddler and seems confused, but she is satisfied to point out the boy's father. The girl's pale skin, blonde hair and lilac dress make her appear faded, like fabric washed too many times. Eli is content with her company only because he knows no better.

The creeping darkness soon makes their work impossible.

They scurry down to shore bellowing bawdy songs and laughter, certain they are prepared for the next morning's trip into the icy ocean. No doubt the same few will retire to pray at the side of the bed while the rest quaff their savings at the inn, traveling as a single entity to shield themselves from the beasties stalking the hillsides.

He catches up with her—the faded fabric, her smile the brightest thing about her—embracing her and the child with simple happiness. The passing men greet her, amused by the unusual display of passion. They stroll home to light a fire in the grate and share a meal caught from the deep. My own stomach rumbles for fish.

I push away from the branch and unfurl my wings, allowing my body to be thrown high over the gray water. I stretch my ebony limbs and feel them bob up and down on the airwaves. My long black hair is pulled in all directions; this is a freedom the villagers would never experience. The wind curls around my exposed nipples and clitoris, stinging them and making them tingle. The water grows darker beneath me, her depths dizzying and home to a thousand mysterious creatures. I need to keep a sharp eye open for all of them.

The water crashes over my body as I dive into a school of mackerel, dragging my net through them and emerging with the squirming bodies. I finally breathe out; I have survived another hunt. I pick up speed until my cliffs are visible through the fog, turning sideways at the entrance and darting between stalactites until I reach a hollow spot in the wall. It looks ready to me; sheepskins line the floor and now there is a pile of flapping fish. I wait, nibbling at one, until each candle in the village would be blown out.

I coast above the rooftops. This hour of starry night is visible only to creatures like me and other beasties. Crawling through the dirt roads and hillocks would be Hobgoblins and Ghouls, their grabbing arms and sharp teeth waiting for any human foolish enough to leave the safety of home. They're crude and obnoxious creatures, their minds always on low things. The stone parish looks on helplessly from the top of the hill.

I grasp the brick roof with hands and feet and scurry down the wall until I reach the window, silently sliding a dewclaw in my wrist underneath the pane. Locks have never been a match for it; each decade there is a new kind but I dispatch it simply and quickly. The sleeping couple doesn't stir, their breathing rhythmic as the sea, soft and even. The room is simple, almost bare, and the stump of a candle sits on a holder atop the cabinet. His head is nestled into the crook of her neck and rage bubbles through my blood. I creep on feet and knuckles toward the bed and he stirs, turning over to face me. His lids flutter open. His brow creases. He sees catlike amber eyes so different from his own, likely floating in the dark due to my blackened skin and his poor night vision. The cotton wool of sleep begins to clear and realization trickles into his expression. I place my hand over his mouth before the shouting begins.

His arms almost squeeze the breath from me as we soar over the crashing tide. His body is rigid and shaking violently. I notice his eyes are shut as the cave envelops us, and he opens them only when I deposit him in the freshly decorated hollow. He shivers amongst the fleeces, the musty scent of sheep still clinging to them. I sit at his feet while he stares at me with eyes like a trapped animal. The sea is audible in the distance.

I offer a fish but he doesn't respond; the whites of his eyes are large circles around the blue. Understanding their feeding habits is tedious; what suits one is never right for another and clearly this bounty will not be acceptable. It's not a concern to me. I tear off a fish's head and chew morosely—they're a fearful species, entirely incapable of grasping new opportunities. After a few moments he finds his voice. "Wh-what are you going to do to me?"

I smile gently but he balks at my pointed teeth. Their dislike of difference can always be relied upon, but I know he will grow used to me. "Surely you've heard the stories." I speak gently, hypnotically.

"You're going to kill me." He speaks with the flatness of certainty. I don't reply; I have learned it is best not to make promises. "Then please, get it done. I don't wish to be your mouse to play with." Elsewhere his sensitive appearance might denote a life of the softest silk against his skin and the sweetest wine on his tongue, but existence in the remote town has toughened him.

"I don't know what you've heard, but that isn't why I've brought you here." He looks almost hopeful. I crawl toward him, slow as a snake, over his legs and torso until my face is a tongue's length from his. His skin smells of the salt air but also of herbs, sweet rosemary and spicy cinnamon. His breath is on my face. "Some of the weaker ones perish it's true, but you seem somewhat sturdier."

He flinches and gathers his strength, pushing me hard away from him. I flutter, strewing feathers over the ground. I abandon him for the coolness of the air outside, leaving him to fume in isolation. I can hear him calling out but he needs time to think, time to let the situation settle. The droplets in the wind sting my face, refreshing me, and I am surprised to feel anger receding. Where had the anger come from? Surely I didn't feel rejected?

The tip of the sun nudges the horizon, sending weak white

ripples over the tide. I glide back into the darkness. His jaw is set. "Please," he says calmly. "I have a family, children, a wife. I could be back before anyone knows."

"You could," I reply, and stretch my body full length next to his, ensuring my nipple strokes his arm. His eyes dart away; in his society only women who roam city streets at night behave this way. He can't resist turning back to my breasts though, taking in the sight of them, the closeness, the warmth he can feel from them. "My nipples are hard," I say, a fact he seems to have noticed already. The pulsing at his crotch is unmistakable and his breathing deepens. I can hear the heartbeat at his throat—my lips are almost touching it. He backs away, curling into the fetal position in the corner.

The hollow grows bright with the sun and dark once again with shadows. A rustling stirs me from the corner I have coiled into. I catch him sniffing at one of the fish before throwing it down again. I watch him a moment longer, his pale face screwing up in disgust, but his hands are unable to stop searching. He's hungry and, while I have sympathy, I know it will make things easier for me. His eyes catch mine and his body stiffens. His expression no longer registers fear, merely quiet caution.

"You want to rejoin the others, don't you?" I say.

"Yes." He speaks with firmness but his eyes lower.

I grunt with frustration. Why am I frustrated? I have only to wait but somehow I feel time is running away. I need to taste him, to bury my face in his hair. "Why is it so important to live your little lives, seeing nothing but the world you were born into?"

He looks back up at me, his delicate features hard. "What's the alternative? Wander, alone and freezing, into the abyss? Let one of the creatures of the night drag me away?"

"Not everywhere is the same as here. There are vast cities where exotic rugs and spices are sold, every color you can think of; and at night the doors to opium dens are opened, where women writhe to music and snakes coil around their bellies."

"Well," he says, keeping his voice even, but he's afraid of pushing me too far, "if these wonderful places exist, why are you here?"

"I have something I need to do." I wave my hand vaguely, annoyed that I'm offering an explanation. "But I have the choice, you see, which makes me less trapped." I realize that while I'm compelled to return to my hatch place for the spawning, I'm drawn here anyway. I ruffle my feathers in irritation. He's spotted a weakness.

"You understand, don't you, how it feels to have a home?" He crawls nearer to me. Now it's my eyes that lower. "Where are the others like you? Do you ever see them?"

I'm disinclined to answer, but I humor him. The words struggle to leave my mouth. "There aren't many. We've devised other means of survival." I see him inflate with satisfaction, and I'm suddenly angry. "What about you? Did you marry the first girl to cross your path, or just someone your parents decided for you?" He looks stung, eyes wide with shock and offense.

"I love Milly," he says quietly. I can see it's true, which infuriates me further.

"And haven't you ever been tempted?" I ask. I unfold my body and lie straight on my side. He tries not to look but his eyes glance all over me. "Haven't you ever looked at another woman and wondered what it might be like?"

This time he's flustered. He trips on his words. "Well, of course but, I mean, I never..." He takes a breath. "Everyone... at times..." He doesn't finish his sentence. He places a hand to his brow and caresses his forehead. "I do wonder. I think about it late at night, when I'm certain my wife is sleeping. I..." He's unwilling to speak, "use my hand sometimes, even after we've already lain together. It's different"—he gazes out at the entrance of the hollow, lost in the scent of strange women and their unknown crevices—"than it is with Milly." The mention of her name brings him back. He looks broken, like a discarded marionette. His admission has left my nipples standing again and my vagina lips feel hot. I want to reassure him, to embrace him. "I'm hungry and tired," he says. "You have to help me. Don't you know how to make fire? How to cook?"

I know of such things but they hold no interest for me. My own stomach rumbles but I don't reach for a fish. Instead I gesture to him. "I will," I say quietly, soothingly, "as soon as we wake." His head falls to his chest, defeated, and he shuffles toward me. His body is slender but strong, with small muscles on his thin arms. I wrap my own arm over him as his back nestles into my stomach. He's weakened, and he falls quickly into a feverish sleep. At first I struggle to remain alert but I, too, join him in obliviousness.

The scrabbling at first invades my dreams—it seems a mouse is struggling to descend the cave wall. Slowly sleep leaves me and I realize what's happening. I throw myself into the dark and hover above Eli as he holds desperately onto the rocks. He is miles above ground, climbing down an endless chasm. His hands shake and his breathing is harsh. I scoop him up and deposit him back to safety, where it takes several minutes for his pulse to slow. I study him. All traces of fear drain away and he lies limply against the wool, eyes half closed. His fight is gone and he knows now he is here for the duration. He is mine.

He doesn't protest this time as I wind my body around his,

mixing our warmth. My wings wrap around him, enclosing him and pulling him tighter. His body is soft and very hot. I flick my tongue over his neck and he moans softly, his erection pressing against my thigh. The scent of rosemary hasn't faded. He opens his eyes, his pupils dark holes, and looks directly into mine. A flush has spread to his cheeks and lips; part hunger, part fever, part need. The pride I feel at inducing such pleasure, at witnessing him in such a private state, sends a fizz of gratification through me. I've forgotten the confusion and sadness of the past—right now I have what I want. "I still love my wife," he murmurs as he reaches for my breasts, stroking them and tugging with gentle fingertips at my nipples.

"I know," I whisper, breathing deeply as the hot waves travel from his touch to my groin. I feel the wetness flow from me and my hands shake with excitement as I untie the string around his trousers, releasing his erection. I grip it eagerly and rotate it slowly back and forth, wetting my fingers with the tip. It grows harder, insistent. I've brought him to this, this moment of absolute need, and I feel the power course through me.

"Mmm," he moans, leaning forward to take my nipple into his mouth. A shot of pain and pleasure darts through me as his teeth pull firmly and I yelp, smiling. Something like lightning shoots through me when he flicks his tongue. I lift myself onto my knees and straddle him, the tip of his erection prodding against the lips of my vagina. I tease him a moment, almost letting him in before rising again. I love to watch his face, his excitement, and my skin prickles as I finally sink him into myself. We sigh together as though we could stay like this for an eternity.

He holds my hips as I buck against him. I feel exposed up here, like he can see all my bad habits, so I grab his left hand

and trace his finger upward along my thigh to my clitoris. Just the hot touch of him there elicits a deep moan of desire and relief from me. He seems pleased but frowns for a moment; the village folk are frustratingly ignorant of such things. I guide him, and when he sees how much I respond he understands. Now I feel his touch from inside too, stroking my deepest point. I grow dizzy and shut my eyes; a wave of pleasure is trickling slowly down my body and into my fingers and toes. The sensation grows and intensifies like a storm building and I know it's coming.

"Oh!" It crashes wildly through me. I grab his shoulder as my body stiffens and shakes, and it bursts through my arms and fingertips and floods my brain. I fall against him, my mouth buried in his neck.

He kisses my shoulder and my heart flutters. I wish I could keep him here with me, but that's just not how it's done. I grip his arms, my face still buried in his neck. The ends of his hair flick against my nostrils when I breathe in, his herbal scent sedating me. I roll against him until his breaths become sighs and his sighs become moans. He grows harder inside me, reaching up farther. With a gasp it's over and, as he spurts into my farthest recesses, I bite down on the pulse of his neck. His wail is high, pure pleasure and pure pain. His expression is both shock and bliss. His semen and his blood gush into me, metallic stickiness coating my tongue and gums, his body both fertilizing the egg I will lay and providing its nutrition.

His heartbeat slows and so do I. I can never bring myself to suck their last breath, feel their body go limp and cold. Instead I pull my lips away and watch the wound congeal, holding him. It's over now, and I feel as alone as the first time. He'll be like Sam now, if he survives, always watching the skies and waiting for my return, for even a glimpse of my black shadow streaking through the clouds. In turn I will continue as before, knowing that a heart waits for me nearby. When the bleeding stops I gather him in my arms, smell his flowery rosemary scent and fly back to the brick houses.

DEVOURED BY ENVY

Jo Wu

Men have always told me that I was too pure. I incited in them a fear that they would despoil something much too innocent.

"You're like a doll," my latest suitor told me one evening. His wide eyes, like those of a frightened fawn, surveyed me from head to toe, drinking in the sight of my waist-length flaxen ringlets, my flushed porcelain cheeks and the frothy white lace gown that cinched my waist. He was not the first one to pay me this compliment, but the flattery did nothing to hide my glassy blue eyes as I willed myself not to blink, lest tears should escape the confines of my lashes.

"Giselle, I adore you, but I can't bring myself to love you the way a man should."

"Why?" I spat, though I already knew the answer. At least five other men shared his sentiment.

"Y-you're too much of an angel," he stammered. "When I see you dance, I...I can't help but to think that...to love you would mean to ruin you, to-to-to..."

I glared at him, daring him to make a final statement.

"To love you would mean the death of you!"

He scampered off into the congested dim streets, abandoning me in the midst of black horse carriages and lovers in their dark evening finery, hustling along for a dance or a drink. I sighed. With my fair dress, skin, and hair, I was like a star traversing through an overcast sky as I made my way home.

My abode is known as Château Angélique de Verre— Angelic Castle of Glass, as everyone in the city calls it. They are right to deem it as such. It is a castle built of rose-colored glass, surrounded by crimson and pink roses that blossom throughout the year. Within the glass walls are vast libraries that smell of tangy ink upon warmly pressed pages that almost feel like the smooth skin of a child, faintly scented with cinnamon. Gardens flourish through numerous halls, green and fragrant with magnolias and lilies. There are even bedrooms fit for queens, complete with canopied beds with satin and silk covers in the richest reds or deepest violets.

I lie alone at night, relishing the slick sensation of silk against my bare legs. A hard, thick book always lies with me, lulling me to dream worlds with the seductive curls of their printed letters. Yet, even with the wide cast of valiant men who lie by my side in their entrapments of fiction, my bed is still cold. I have no real man of bone and blood, skin and hair, by my side. No reassurance of solid muscles to encase me with affections as I lie beneath a sea of silk.

In spite of my loneliness, every evening at precisely seven o'clock, I am the city's primary source of entertainment. I have been deemed the brightest star of the city's nightlife, a snow-white rose that blooms in the evening. When I pirouette upon my steel toes, and the spotlight plays with the scintillating diamonds upon my bodice, the entire audience gawks at me as a little girl would upon a ballerina figurine that twirls in her music box. I perform with nothing but the energy that surges in my costumed body and the painted backdrops to fool the audience into believing that a fairy tale lives before their eyes, if only for a few hours every evening.

Lately, a young man caught my eye in the front row of the theater. He was always alone. He had neatly trimmed brown hair and a clean-shaven face. His dark eyes turned up at the corners, almost like cat's eyes, and a youthful grin hinted at how he might have looked as a boy. He was well stationed in life, conveyed by the sharp cut of his black suits, sometimes adorned with touches of blue and gold at his cravat.

The evening I learned his name, he was the only one to toss a scarlet rose upon the stage. A note was secured to the stem with an ivory ribbon.

> *Would you accept my invitation for a moonlit stroll? I would take much pleasure in becoming acquainted with the woman behind the enchanting performer.*
>
> *Ever yours,*
> *Dr. Gabriel Blackburn*

Thus began our courtship. It wasn't long before he paid visits to Château Angélique de Verre. Given the maze-like structure of my home, we played hide-and-seek, as if we were once again children. However, our games were laced with carnal sweetness. He would sometimes snatch me by the waist as I hid among the white tulips and marigolds, cover my eyes as he snuck up behind me in the library, or part my lips with his tongue as he pressed me upon a carpet.

However, we had yet to consummate our infatuation.

The evening I planned to lose my virginity, I slipped into a scarlet dress that bared my shoulders. The fabric was so sheer, it revealed more than a mere silhouette of my figure. I relished Gabriel's reaction when I seated him in the dining hall. He had no control over the coughs or chuckles or the blush that bled into his cheeks as he remarked, "Giselle... You're wearing a... a...um, a..."

"A dress?" I giggled like a naive schoolgirl.

"Yes, a dress!" He glanced down upon his empty plate. Like a shy schoolboy unsure of how to answer a teacher, he mumbled, "You... You look...beautiful."

He thought I couldn't hear him. I reached out and curved my slender fingers beneath his chin. He had no choice but to meet my eyes.

"What did you say?" I sweetly asked.

His large Adam's apple bounced like a wine cork in a filled glass.

"You're beautiful."

I squeezed his chin more firmly. "Tell me how beautiful."

"Your hair...it's as golden as the sun—"

"Ha! How unoriginal!" My nails dug into his skin. He clenched his teeth, but the curves that teased the corners of his lips betrayed his amusement. "Hair like mine is always compared to the sun. Or gold or honey. I would appreciate an exercise of your"—the joints of my fingers turned white. My nails nearly drew blood from his jaw—"imagination and creativity."

He chuckled. His large hands stroked and snaked up the

arm that imprisoned his chin. He started with my wrist. Soon, he reached my shoulder, relishing the silky skin beneath his grooved palms. His dark eyes never left mine.

"You are a pearl from the dark confines of the violent ocean, an embodiment of purity amidst our ruined world. A pearl, a paragon to be cherished."

His fingertips probed the thin skin stretched over my hard yet delicate collarbones.

"Do you know those moments of fleeting beauty?" he continued. "I think of a rosebud, so tightly closed, how bulbous it looks, tapering to a narrow tip, like the pucker of a pair of lips. Ah, I believe moments of such shyness are when a rose is the most beautiful. Once it blossoms and splays open its petals without shame for all the world to see, allowing the world to violate it with their eyes and shears, it becomes tarnished and vulgar."

I gasped. His hands flew to the sides of my neck. He then slid his hands upward so that his fingers combed against the back of my scalp.

"I think of your lips as a rosebud." His whisper felt like the flutter of a feather upon my lips. Suddenly, his nails dug into my scalp. He pulled my face closer to him, so that our noses, but not our lips, caressed.

"Kiss me," I ordered in barely more than a gasp.

Our kiss may have bridged our tongues, but the rest of our bodies were still firmly rooted in our chairs. I would have abandoned my seat for his yearning lap, but a bell rang to signal dinner. Regaining propriety, we ate in relative silence. The slick bloody juices of the tender steak made me wonder how I would taste to him.

When he swallowed his final morsel, my hands pounced

upon his to lead him to one of my favorite bedchambers. It looked like a garden with fireflies flittering all around the fragrant green foliage that composed the walls. A waterfall generously gushed down one wall, creating a stream by the bed, which looked like a giant water lotus, large enough to cradle a pair of lovers.

I imagined kissing Gabriel as we both fell upon the lotus petals. Because he was considerably taller than I was, I cupped his face between my hands and rose to the tip of my toes, intending to pull his lips down upon mine.

"Giselle, please, no."

He gently pushed me. I could not help but to topple backward and land upon the bed alone, my mouth slack with surprise. The sheer fabric of my red dress clung to my skin, doing nothing to hide my erect nipples. I brushed away my momentary shock by flashing him a smile, which I meant to be seductive.

He only coughed into his fist.

"Giselle, dear, don't you find your conduct a touch too bold?"

"Don't you *dear* me!" I slapped the air and laughed. "I shall feel as though we've shrunken into married old prunes if you address me so!"

"But we cannot share a bed without the blessing of marriage," Gabriel replied. "I haven't given you a ring!"

"Oh, are you intending to propose, Doctor?"

Gabriel did not look at me. His muteness smudged away my smile. I closed my legs and crossed my arms.

"Gabriel?" I drew myself before him. "Gabriel, what's wrong?"

His dark eyes gazed at nothing upon the floor. He took a deep breath.

"Giselle… I cannot marry you."

A frown yanked my face. "Why not?"

"You are too perfect. The entire city speaks of you in such a way. You must be an angel from the heavens, a star out of reach in the night sky. When you perform every night, you captivate everyone."

"But doesn't that make me all the more desirable?" I touched Gabriel's warm cheek. He flinched, but was otherwise still. "How am I out of reach? You know I am infatuated with you, Gabriel!"

"I am indeed a lucky man to court you, Giselle. But…I fear…the entire city, in fact, fears that, because you are so immaculate, to deflower you would ruin you!"

"What is this nonsense?" I snatched my hand away from him. "How would I be ruined?"

"Your purity is the appeal of your performance," explained Gabriel, now meeting my eyes. "Losing your virginity, whether you're married or not, would mean destroying your appeal to audiences."

"Then why did you court me?"

I clenched my teeth like a dog challenging an opponent, daring Gabriel to explain, or better yet, profess his love.

Instead, he coughed again.

"I was engaged before I gave you that rose."

I widened my eyes. "You were?"

"The engagement was called off. The pain of losing her was so great, I thought courting the famous ballerina would help me forget her."

"But it didn't," I snapped.

His Adam's apple throbbed like a heart beating in desperate need of respiration. "She and I are still very much in love. I admit, there were many times when I pretended that you were her when I kissed you—"

"I was only a plaything to ease your pain, wasn't I?" I snarled.

"Giselle—"

"Get out! Get out and return to her if that's what you want!"

He thinned his lips. He turned away, not needing my guidance to slip out into the evening streets.

In the following evenings, during my performances, Gabriel no longer sat in the front row. I spotted him perched high up in a balcony, seated by a round-faced young woman with slanted dark eyes. She had lustrous black hair elaborately braided and pinned, and her skin was the hue of lightly toasted almonds. I did not find her attractive, but she had the effervescent grin of a young girl, able to provoke Gabriel to laugh at ease. He had a sense of comfort that I never witnessed when he was in my company.

The city newspapers announced that their engagement was official. The evening of the announcement, during my performance, anger ripped through my body, causing me to slip as I split my legs into a long leap. Upon my landing, my toes brushed against the hard stage floor, failing to provide foundation. I screamed as I swung my arms in desperate frenzy and collapsed on my back.

The audience gasped. Yet, the orchestra continued galloping through their music sheets as I bit back my tears. I smiled as I leapt back to my feet, to make believe that the mistake had never occurred, that I really was as immaculate as the entire city believed me to be.

It was when I slipped out into the evening streets through the theater's back door in my heavy coat that I let the trickling tears brand my cheeks with overt shame.

When I arrived home, I was surprised to find a man standing before the entrance with a book of poetry. He was sharply dressed in a black suit and a midnight cloak. As I came closer, he raised his face.

"Gabriel?" I asked.

He stepped into the dim glow of a lamppost, his grin glistening like pearls. Despite the almost twin-like resemblance, he was not Gabriel. His skin was slightly darker, and his jawline was pricked with black stubble. His eyes were not brown. Instead, they were bright green, glinting like absinthe by the light of a flickering fire. Gabriel may have been handsome with the charms of a gentle youth, but this stranger had a feral rawness to him that made my shoulders clench.

As he gave me a low bow, he grasped my hand and kissed it. His stubble tickled me, and his full lips were soft, like warm velvet.

"You're not Gabriel," I said.

He leaned closer to me. "Would you like me to be him?"

His whisper left a lump in my throat. I wanted to say yes. I wanted Gabriel to encase me in his arms, to slip a ring on my finger and brand me as his carnal property.

"You look like him," I told the stranger.

He grinned. "I can show you the proper way a man can love you, more than he ever can."

I wrinkled my nose and brushed past him to unlock my door. "Sir, you are trespassing upon my time and home. I wish you a good night!"

I shut the door behind me. But when I turned, there he was

again! In my hall! His green eyes stabbed me as I backed away. Before I could scream, he remarked, "You do understand the feeling of being lonely, do you?"

"Wha-what is it to you?"

"Who do you envy?"

There was such compassion in his voice. It was like the mew of a kitten in need of shelter during a snowstorm.

"Gabriel's fiancée." I could not help but blurt it. I thought of how beautiful she actually looked sitting next to Gabriel, dressed in a violet gown, her black hair adorned with opals. I held my breath as my heart felt as though metal clamps were compressing it, clawing into it with nails, making it bleed.

His breath licked my neck, almost as slick as a sliding tongue. "Why do you envy her?"

"Because she'll marry him." I felt as though a thick rope had looped around my neck, forbidding me to breathe, to speak, to cry.

Another blast of warm breath against my neck. He purred, "What else?"

"She'll sleep with him." Now a tear slipped past a blinking eye.

The tear was suddenly kissed away. His lips caressed my cheek like a butterfly fleetingly perched upon a dewdrop.

"She'll share his bed, and you fear you'll forever be denied conjugal bliss, don't you, Giselle?" The stranger stroked my hair, his warm fingers long and strong, capable of strangling me. "He'll touch her the way he touched you, but will touch her in ways beyond what he's ever dreamed of doing to you."

One finger lightly traced the smooth outer whorl of my left ear. "She'll share his bed with him every night, as both his pretty little wife and as his wanton whore, hungry for his fingers and whatever secret crevice they may explore."

I thought of how much this stranger resembled Gabriel—his height, his bone structure, his nose, his lips, the shape of his eyes.

"Are you related to Gabriel?"

He smirked as he shook his head.

"I've never seen you in this city before. Are you new?"

"I'm an emotion that strikes every person in the world. I look different to everyone, but I enjoy paying visits when I am called on, particularly if my hosts are suffering broken hearts, unrequited love, and betrayal."

I narrowed my eyes. "What is your name?"

"Envy."

I felt breathless as I continued to stare into his eyes. Green with envy. Green-eyed monster.

"Are you real?"

He chuckled. "You feel me, don't you? I'm throbbing in your veins as you think of that woman sitting by his side. I'm eating you alive as you can hardly breathe knowing that she quenches his desire in ways you can't. I lie by your side every night as you crave a man like me to shower you with kisses."

He kissed my cheek. His lips seared me like glowing iron. His touch caused streams of warmth to course through my veins, prompting my breath to heave. He smiled at me again, his teeth straight and white. "No one but you will ever see me."

Rising to the tips of my toes, I pecked his lips. His eyes flashed with a surge of glinting pleasure. Hooking his arms around my torso, he jerked me closer. My waist collided with his pelvis.

"Would you like me to show you what pleasures Gabriel would grant on his wedding night?"

A lump grew in my throat. I thought of how Gabriel's large hands would imprint me if we married. I thought of how I would wrap my calves around his waist, how he would sound if he were to enter me for the first time. Would he moan and roar or purr words of eternal love? In my reverie, my heart sank as I realized I would never find out. Only his fiancée would discover the secrets I longed to know.

I pressed my head against Envy's shoulder. "Yes, please."

What followed was a blur of roughness as he cupped my face between both of his hands and yanked it up for a voracious kiss. My feet dangled inches above the floor as he embraced me, imbibing my breath with such thirst. He climbed the many stories of my home, stripping my coat, dress, corset lacings and chemise as easily as slicing the curling skin off a ruby apple. I was fully nude when he reached the room where I had planned to give Gabriel my virginity. The waterfall roared as Envy and I crashed upon the lotus bed. My body curved within the contours of the petals, and he shoved away the curtain of hair that shrouded me, stripping my breasts of their last shreds of modesty.

Envy bent over me, drinking in the sight of my vulnerability, relishing the honor of being the first man to see me so exposed. I felt a foreign sensation of constriction between my legs.

"Are you scared?" whispered Envy.

I bit my lip. I had never seen a nude man. His erection was thick and riddled with bulging veins like a maze of wires. I failed to fathom how something so long could fully enter me without stabbing my intestines, how such girth could manage to squeeze into such narrow space. To top it all off, the tip of his member was bulbous, tapering into a sharp tip, like a knife.

"How will that fit inside me?" I hunched my shoulders away from him, though my legs hung open.

He softened my brows with a kiss. "It will hurt, but it won't last."

As he lowered his body between my bent knees, I wrapped my arms around him. Without warning, he nipped my neck. I gasped with little gusts of ecstasy as he traced his incisors down the curve of my neck and over the tip of one of my breasts, trailing red territorial bite marks along the way.

Envy pinned my arms above my head with one hand. His other hand ran up and down the length of his shaft.

"You will feel pain, dear Giselle," he warned. "But it will soon be over."

I could feel the tip of his member now probing my slit. I was soaking with molten desire. Yet, he did not enter me. With his hand wrapped around the base of his penis, he kept thrusting the tip against my wetness, colliding with my throbbing clitoris.

"You're too big!" I whimpered, lamenting that I was a failure as a woman, that I was too small, too tight. No wonder I failed to inspire lust in men.

"Wait," murmured Envy. "Wait, Giselle." With his knees, he pushed my legs wider. Years of flexibility permitted my muscles to stretch, but my bones creaked. Envy spread my wet cavern open with his fingers. He thrust two, three, four and then, with slightly more difficulty, five fingers into me. His fingers curled and thrust within me, drawing slick juices as one would draw water from a pumping well.

"You're so small, so tight," Envy remarked with a chuckle. "But you're a precious commodity. You haven't been pillaged by other men."

He drew out his damp fingers. Still pinning my arm with his other hand, he grasped the base of his erection once again. He moved slowly, as if fearing that he would startle me, that he would transform from a lover to a predator.

I screamed. I bucked my head against the bed beneath me as I felt a popping pain like the stab of a dagger.

"Did it go in?" I shrieked.

With a forward thrust of Envy's hips, I felt the smooth sensation of him gliding into me.

I gasped. "It... It went in?"

Envy slid his member out of me. Or most of it. I felt a sudden tugging at my opening. He tugged once, and then a second time. He pulled once again, but with a great yank.

I screamed and jolted beneath him, as if needles stuck me. I could not help but realize a slack emptiness where there was once unsullied tightness. I breathed heavily and remained still within the curve of the giant petal as I stared at Envy. He was gasping for breath as well, but pleasure and pride gleamed in his eyes.

"You're bleeding," he remarked.

I glanced at his erection. It glistened with trickles of crimson droplets. The tip glistened like a ruby. The burning juices of my arousal felt no different from blood, so Envy dipped a finger into my gash. He brought his fingertip before my eyes, showing me the blood that gleamed like scarlet dew.

"Don't stop," I whimpered.

He thrust into me again. He pinned both of my wrists over my head as he came into me again and again, drawing spurts of blood. My moans and screams must have been a symphony to him. They vibrated along with the crashes of the waterfall and the gurgling of the stream. At the climax, Envy roared as he dug his nails into my hips, stabbing me over and over, leaving me with bruises that bloomed like black roses as his viscous ejaculations flooded out of me, mixing with rivers of my blood.

At the end of it all, my legs trembled and dripped with his seed and my blood. When Envy cradled me in his arms and carried me out of the room, I caught a glimpse of the water lotus bed. Streaks and splotches of blood defiled it, displaying incriminating evidence of my defloration.

Perhaps Gabriel was right. Perhaps the loss of my virginity would lead to my ruin. At my performance the evening after my intimacy with Envy, my legs quivered from the shuddering soreness Envy's weight inflicted on them. I could not kick as high as I normally would, nor could I twirl as fluidly. Audience members even gasped at the conspicuous bruises on my pale skin, like black spots on a white dog's fur.

"A horrid performance indeed!" quipped an old woman as she traipsed out of the theater with her friend. "It was like watching a little girl pretending to dance!"

Hearing the wedding bells ringing for Gabriel and his bride did nothing to alleviate my bitterness. On their wedding day, I caught a glimpse of them riding through the city in a crimson carriage, waving to the cheering passersby as the bride's veil fluttered behind her like a white flag—a flag that signaled her surrender of virginity to the man I desired.

There was an evening when no one came to my performance. As I stormed through the city streets, I spotted Gabriel and his wife clinking their wine glasses by the glow of candles through the window of a restaurant. Shrouded by the shadows of the streets, I fled home.

When I arrived back at Château Angélique de Verre, there was Envy, sitting upon a chaise lounge with crossed legs, enjoying a glass of absinthe. He glanced up at me, his eyes the same hue as his beverage.

"The city no longer cares for me," I spat at him. "They couldn't care less if I died."

Envy stroked my hair and kissed my brow.

"At least you'll always be with me." I felt like a lost child as I threw my arms around him, pressing my cheek to his chest. "You won't ever leave me, will you?"

"As long as you dwell on your losses, I will always be yours, sweet little Giselle." Envy rested his cheek atop my head. He rubbed my back. I didn't want his kindness. I felt angry. Resentment raced through my veins, lusting for an outlet to explode.

"Take me, Envy," I ordered. "I'm yours to do with what you will."

He whisked me to the library. A large black birdcage sat hidden between two shelves, with a chair inside to provide a comfortable reading spot amidst the maze of books. After tearing off my clothes, Envy threw my body over the side of the chair. My stomach pressed against the soft velvet. I could have hung my head, but Envy gripped my hair like the reins of a horse. I screamed and moaned as he yanked me back, slowly easing into me, filling me with every inch of him.

"You like this, do you, Giselle?"

He yanked harder on my hair, ramming his girth into me. His nails drew blood from my waist as he gripped me and thrust harder. It was not long before I felt him loop ropes around my wrists. I was suddenly yanked up to my toes. He tied both of my wrists to the bars of the cage. My hands were raised above my head, forming a V. Envy then looped a cord around one of my ankles. Because I was flexible enough, he tied the rope to the top of the cage so that my foot was raised high above my head. My other leg was left dangling.

"Perfect for penetration," he remarked, grinning at his handiwork.

I felt sharp pain as my wet opening widened for him. It was as if I was a virgin again. He clutched my throat and thrust into me. As his hands burned around my neck, my thoughts flew to Gabriel and his wife, who would surely enjoy a night of pleasure after their dinner. I thought of the emptiness of my theater.

"No one will miss me out there, will they?" I murmured.

Envy paused mid-thrust, his member only halfway in me, slick with my desire.

"No. They won't." His absinthe eyes stung my skin. "You're safe in this castle of glass. This is your world. Our world."

Millions of pages throughout the library fluttered like doves' wings as my screams vibrated from within the black cage. I doubt anyone in the streets took heed of the thin scratches that began to slice the glass walls as my voice rang.

THE HARDEST KISS

Cairde Glass

𝕭ás led the young man between the damp walls, past doors that belched little clouds of laughter and lantern glow, through sticky puddles to a cul-de-sac between buildings. It was dark and smelled like piss and soot-clouded rain, but it was private and that was what mattered. Moonlight spilled over the intermingling rooftops and fell in a splash of silver across the steep incline of the lad's forehead and the rough wedge of his nose.

The boy, Luke he'd called himself, wetted his lips with his tongue, then wiped them with his shirt cuff. "Here?"

Bás nodded, remembered Luke could not see him in the dark and stepped closer. "Yes. Here."

"You want I should go first?" His hands found Bás, groping downward till his fingers rested on the cold metal of the older man's belt buckle.

"No." He leaned forward till the cool light of the moon reflecting off the lad's sallow face filled his eyes. "I shall start."

The kiss was light. Not delicate, for Bás was not. Nor gentle.

But he held the lad the way a lover might and laid his lips against the thin mouth with a measure of fondness. It was the one thing he remembered clearly. Not love. Neither lust. But there were, after all, many kinds of intimacy and this always seemed sufficient.

Luke grew bolder, deepening the exchange, and Bás allowed him that liberty. *The end comes soon.* Already the young man burned, his body growing weak as his passion swelled. "Sir." His voice crackled like ash. "I know you." His eyes stammered back and forth. "But I dun' know you. How is that?"

Bás stroked Luke's hair and rocked him like a child. "You know the idea of me. All men do. From birth, they know the idea of me."

The lad coughed—his lips flecked with blood. "Think I'm dying, sir."

"Aye."

"Stay wi' me? Till the end?" His eyes were wide and white behind the lank fringe of his hair.

Bás nodded. "That's why I came to you."

Luke frowned. "Ah." Understanding dawned. "Tha's all right, then." He coughed again, dribbled blood and wiped it clumsily away with his sleeve. "Will it hurt?"

"Naw. Like going to sleep it'll be." He shook his head and cupped the young man's face in his hands. "Now. Kiss me, boy."

The kiss was hard. The last kiss always was. Luke's soul filled Bás's mouth, crowding down his throat and burning in his chest. The boy fell to the ground empty, his flesh resembling a discarded vessel, at home in the midst of the rain barrels and rats.

Bás coughed and spat, legs trembling with the aftershock. Warmth coursed through him, and he flexed his fingers, tingling instead of numb. But the heat faded as the soul settled into his belly.

It was time to visit the gate. He felt bloated—heavy with the dead, like having gorged on old meat or drunk from the tap until the keg was empty and he was sickened by it. And covetous. It was the point at which he felt the most alive; it allowed him the fantasy of being human again.

Rain splatted on the shingles overhead, stray drops finding their way into the fissure of the alley. Bás turned up his coat collar out of habit. The rain would not make him any colder than he already was. Cold as the winter air. And in the summer he burned, hot and thick and smothering. Being wet made little difference. But there was an instinct, a shadow of the man he used to be, that turned up his collar and hunched his shoulders against the rain.

The street was empty, night and the weather keeping even indecent folk inside. He strolled unhindered toward the underground terminal. Candles flickered against the walls, each a prayer to the gods asking for money or health or simply life. The flames danced as he walked past and a scabby woman held out her hands, one empty, the other gripping a dirty candle stub. Bás shook his head. He had no need for money or health, and life, something he longed for, would never be granted.

Treading down the rusting steps, he stepped into the trembling belly of the gear-car. The conductor, standing in the far door of the car, checked his watch and nodded to the engineer. "Tha'll be it. Take us home."

Bás settled into an empty seat, the car shaking underfoot as the gears in the chassis were engaged with the screw that would drive them down the track. There was no need to watch for his exit. There was only one stop to be made—the last one.

The maintenance cavern was a billowing, screeching mass of furnaces and steam and coal dust. The shovelers trudged back and forth, skin sweat-slick under the stiff leather aprons, pushing barrows of coal from bin to fire and returning empty to start over again. One or two looked up with a shudder as Bás walked by, red-ringed eyes going wide behind the thick glass of their goggles. He smiled and shook his head to each of them. Their time was soon, but not yet.

Beyond the cavern was a tunnel leading down into the earth. A bore-hole through the rock, it only just accommodated the span of his shoulders. Wriggling and cursing he came out on the other side into a second cavern, darker and emptier save for the gate.

The gate.

It squatted in the shadows like a scrap-yard dog. Massive girders ran ceiling to floor, like the limbs of a fallen tree, some standing strong, some wilting toward the uneven ground. Pipes wound over and around, broken stubs dribbling hot water and oil. Steam chuffed out in rank clouds at his approach, gears beginning to turn until the bars drew back and the gate flung open. Beyond was uncertain darkness that rippled like water. Or fire.

Out of that darkness came something more monstrous than flame. "You are late." Aithan's voice was irritable.

Bás dropped to his knees. "I'm sorry, master. The last one..."

"No excuses. Show me what you've brought."

Bás's stomach roiled and he vomited out the souls he had consumed earlier. They swirled like bits of leaf caught in a gutter, drifting toward the gate and vanishing into the murk beyond. He wiped a dribble of bile from his chin. Once or twice he had tried to hold on to one, desperate to keep that feeling of being full and alive. But, always, it had torn free, leaving him an empty mass of flesh that lived beyond death. He grinned, mirthless. *Beyond death.* If only that were true.

"That is all you have brought?" Aithan's voice drove the smile from his face. "Hardly enough to keep me waiting this long."

"Please, master. I took all that you instructed me to."

"Insufficient." His hand gripped Bás by the collar. "You will be punished."

"No, sir. I can't." He might be dead, but he was not beyond pain any more than he was beyond winter's chill or summer's heat.

"Do not argue with me or I will double that which you receive." Aithan shook him like a man with a dog. "But I am tired. You will spend the night thinking on your shortcomings and the just punishment you deserve."

Bás whimpered and squeezed his lips shut. It would do no good to beg for mercy. It never did.

Aithan dragged him into the shadows where a door stood wedged in the rock. It was not like the gate; there was nothing supernatural about it, but Bás shivered. There was the shriek of the key in the lock, the answering scream of rusted hinges. He dropped hard onto his knees as Aithan's hand propelled him into the room beyond, preferring that to running face-first into the rough wall. The door rang like a poorly forged bell, water shaking loose from the slick walls in a splatter of dirt and cold. Then he was alone.

Bás covered his head with his arms and swallowed back tears with the same determination as he held down a bellyful of souls. He would not lend his master the knowledge of the depths of his fear. Settling in the center of the room, he tried to calm himself for sleep.

Perhaps if he had a bed it'd be simpler, but the room was nothing more than an old cistern; rough walls spiraling up and up from the muddy bottom. On clear nights he sometimes saw stars or a snippet of the moon. On stormy nights there was only darkness and the uneven fall of rain on his bare head.

He propped elbows on knees, chin on hands and tried to think of nothing. The dread of the punishment to come in the morning ate at him.

"A pox," he whispered. "On Aithan, master of the underworld." The words were cold in his mouth. His master was immortal and there was no pox that could touch him, no matter how much Bás might wish it. "A pox on the mother who bore me and the father who fed me. May sickness visit those who let me live until I fell into the clutches of the many-cursed Aithan." The thought warmed him. In the early days it had been guilt that fired up in his heart with the proclamations, but it had slowly grown into the heat of spite. If he was to be miserable, he would not be the only one.

One of the copper tubes that snaked into the cistern from distant rooftops rattled and clanged and a small, hard thing dropped from the opening and pinged off the stone wall. Then another, splashing into the mud. And another.

Bás pushed back against the door as the darkness buzzed. Something crept over his hand. "Get off." He shook it away, but another one landed in his hair, on his cheek. Tiny metal feet scritched across his clothes and there was the tickling kiss of mesh wings against his face.

Beetles.

He moaned, certain it was another of Aithan's torments, but shut his lips against the scream burning in his throat. If he didn't struggle, perhaps they would be quick. The hair on his body stood up as dozens, then hundreds of little metal bugs covered him. He waited, barely breathing, for them to bite or sting or crawl down his throat. The hum of wings grew louder—the same cheerful dissonance as a calliope. His clothing pulled tight and his feet lifted from the ground.

They swung back and forth, like a small boat burdened with too many passengers, then steadied and began to rise. Bás glanced down. Blackness yawned between his feet and he shut his eyes, hard. Once or three times he felt his hand brush the hard-slick wall of the cistern, but the crash he was expecting did not come.

Smoke and mud tinged the air. Then wind touched his face and he opened his eyes, cautious. The city careened below his feet, a mush of gray and shadows and fire.

The beetle cloud dragged him swiftly among chimneys, over the hill and crest of rooftops until they came to rest on a balcony, the railing blooming with rust. The bugs drifted away like ash and Bás stepped into the house.

It was dark and smelled of rot. A fire burned dull in the grate, spitting a bit of coal onto the hearthstone with a derogatory hiss. Then, silence. And the sound of water running. *A bath.* Not simply running, but running over. Dread settled in his chest and he pushed open the door, expecting to see someone sunk to the bottom of the tub. Slipped, perhaps, and drowned. Or fallen asleep and also drowned.

The girl was neither. If he had been someone else, if the water trickling across the floor had not been rusty with blood, he might have thought she was asleep. It was so strong a feeling that he stayed in the doorway, afraid to make a sound that would wake her.

She stirred, water rippling down the side of the tub in russet threads, and opened her eyes. "Bás." Her voice was broken. "You have come."

A sliver of unease cut through him. "How do you know my name, lady?"

"You don't remember?"

"Remember what?"

She shook her head. "It doesn't matter." A crook of her fingers. "Come here."

He hesitated. It felt wrong to be looking at her; his hands shook at the idea of touching her. "Lady, I should not." But his legs moved, step by slow step across the wet floor.

"Should not?" Her voice mocked him.

"Cannot..." He paused. "I don't remember how to take a woman in my arms or the secret places that make her moan and tremble."

Her fingers traced lightly down the front of his shirt, circling once over his crotch before she gripped him firmly. "Yes, you do," she said. The palm of her hand rubbed against him, warm and tempting.

"Reflex," Bás whispered.

"I'll help you with the rest."

"No." He stepped away. "My body is scarred. And cold. Hardly fit to touch or...please you." It was not merely Aithan's spite that sent him to collect souls at night; his service as death had taken a hard toll.

She rose and wrung the water from her hair. Her skin was copper and milk, flawless except for the ragged slash on her left arm. Blood oozed from the wound, sluggish. She stepped out of the tub, and he watched as water dripped from the dark curls between her legs, trickling down the curve of her thighs, down the slender column of her legs to puddle on the dull floor. "If you do not want me..."

"I do." The words came out as a groan and Bás took another step back. "I want you like breath, like daylight. Like life. But you deserve better."

"Ahh." She sighed. "That is where you are wrong."

"Why?"

"You will understand soon." She held out her hands, warm as daylight. "Please, Bás."

A shudder ran through him and he closed his eyes, trying to remember the things he had forgotten. "Tell me your name."

"Sephie." Her breath curled against his cheek and he twitched.

"Sephie."

A gentle tug at his feet and he opened his eyes to see she knelt to unfasten his shoes. "No." Sephie looked at him, questioning. "You will dirty your hands. Let me." He squatted on the cracked marble and pulled at the buckles. Shame bowed his head and desire raised his eyes so that he caught little glimpses of her—the tight swell of a nipple, the curve of her mouth, the supple skin of her belly.

The worn stitching on his trousers creaked with the strain as his blood continued to rise. Trembling, Bás stood and shed his worn clothes, hands drifting, awkward, in an attempt to cover the raw skin on his knees, the hard welts on his back.

"Your master is unkind." Sephie laid her hand against his chest and warmth trickled across his skin.

He ducked his head, embarrassed. "You deserve..."

She stopped him with a kiss, letting him taste the life in

her. "Come lie with me." Her fingers twined with his and she drew him into the darkened bedroom and down onto the bed. She filled his arms comfortably, holding him close and opening herself to him. He kissed the soft skin between her breasts and then the firm pearls of her nipples and she sighed. The warmth from her hands soothed the aching scars on his back and he took a breath, no longer touched with pain. "Ah, Sephie." He murmured her name against the smooth curve of her belly. The taste of her—sweet as an autumn apple—clung to his tongue as he delved the wetness of her folds, opening and exploring the heat of her with his mouth. She shuddered when he touched the hard knot at the crest of her mound and knotted her fingers tight in his hair with a whimper. He licked her and watched the blood rushing beneath her skin—blooming gently in her cheeks and drawing her nipples erect. His flesh ached, hungry for the warmth and sweetness that his mouth had found. Still he hesitated. His body was like winter; to make love to him was to make love with ice.

Uncertain, Bás slipped a finger into her. Sephie gasped, but rocked against his hand, pressing him deeper inside. "Ohh." She moaned as he stroked her, teasing her sweet spot. A shiver ran through her, and her hands tightened, then loosened in his hair.

"Bás." Her voice broke with need. "Please."

Her eyes widened as they came together, but her legs wrapped tight around his waist, pulling him in. "Sephie." It was a curse. And a prayer. Her cunt gripped him tight, trembling around his shaft while she writhed in slow ecstasy.

Bás matched her rhythm, pushing into her deeply with even strokes. It was all he was capable of, tongue caught hard between his teeth as he shuddered on the edge of climax. He could feel her heart, fluttering rapid against his chest, hear the catch in her breath with every thrust. *She is close.* But his own need had him teetering a hairsbreadth from release.

Sephie pulled his mouth down to hers, teasing his lips open with her tongue, then slipping it into his mouth. He groaned and shook as he spilled inside her and she came with him— arching beneath him, then wilting slowly onto the bed.

For a moment he lay still, head resting between her breasts. It seemed familiar. Not just being with a woman, but being with her, and he shivered, cold and sick. "Sephie?" he said, reluctant.

"Mmm." She pushed a bit of hair back from his forehead. "Bás." His name fell from her mouth like wine and he shut his eyes, giddy.

"I feel I know you. But I do not. How is that?" His voice cracked, fearful.

"You do not remember? Perhaps that is for the best," she whispered.

Rising onto his elbows, he looked at her. For a moment he saw her with sun in her hair, hands filled with summer flowers. "What don't I remember? Why?" Then, with the taste of certainty bitter on the back of his tongue, "Aithan will punish me for this."

"No." Drawing him back down, she smoothed the strain from his shoulders. "He will not touch you ever again." But there was sorrow in her eyes.

"Don't be sad," he said.

She licked her lips and cupped his face in her hands. "Kiss me, Bás."

The kiss was hard. The last kiss always was. He struggled as his soul forced its way home, then he wilted against her. In his chest his heart stirred and beat, his lungs filled and emptied.

Sephie smiled and laid him on the bed, combing his hair neatly around his face. It wasn't within her power to heal his wounds, but life already returned some of the beauty he had lost in service to Aithan. "He will suffer for what he did." She whispered it so he would not wake. There was a buzz and rattle at the window—metal feet tapping against the glass. Throwing back the curtains, she opened the casing and the beetles swarmed in. They washed up against her feet like the ocean and retreated as quickly, milling on the floor and in the air. Confusion chittered around the room and a pane in the window cracked.

"Silence," she said. The clockwork things stopped, a handful of them pinging sharply on the floor as they dropped out of the air. "You came at my summons. You will do as I say."

The beetles scritched against the floor, uneasy.

"I'll deal with Aithan. You take Bás to the place he called home." She waved a hand. "Now, please."

They rustled up from the floor, buzzing and whirring. One by one they alighted on the bed and drew the sheet up in tiny claws until Bás swung between them. Shimmering like a bit of fog, they went out the window and the room was silent.

Sephie fingered the scar on her arm, already healing despite the blood that had been lost. Six years she had spent in the mortal coil, lying in the bed with the molting canopy, neither sleeping nor waking. Nor dead. Simply waiting. She rubbed her throat, still raw. Aithan had tricked her, giving her the pomegranate. *My favorite.* The seeds had clogged in her throat, ruining her voice and stealing her magic. *But no more.*

She buttoned her dress, then sat on the edge of the bed and fastened her shoes. Her hair was no longer wet but a moment of playing with it—pulling it up into a knot, twisting it on one side of her head—made it clear there was no point in trying to contain it. The curls would be loose by her next breath. She pushed it behind her ears and stood.

The vial of pomegranate seeds sat on the dresser, like blood-stained teeth waiting to be traded in for a coin. Sephie nestled it in the bodice of her dress, a cold weight between her breasts to remind her of what was at stake. *Vengeance.*

She pulled back the drapery on the wall, releasing a cloud of dust that nearly choked her. The dull brass grate of the lift was stiff, but after a hard shove it folded out of the way and she stepped into the tiny elevator. Her hair drifted around her face as a breath of air swirled up from below. A turn of the wheel beside the latticed door did nothing and she stamped her foot, impatient. "Down."

Magic flowed, touching not only the lift but the entire house. It shook, plaster falling from the ceiling in chunks and splattering on the floor like ash, and the thing began to sink, the night outside the window pushed upward by the blackness of underground.

She dropped to her knees, arms over her head as the house fell and fell apart. The noise was terrible. Glass shattered and the brick facing scraped against the raw earth outside with a hideous shriek. The roof cracked open, raining tiles on the marble floor. Down and down with noise and dust and the lift car shuddering like something dying. She screamed and covered her eyes, waiting for the impact at the bottom.

Silence nearly flattened her.

Cautious, she raised her head.

Blue-green light moved like water on the mossy ground, spilling from drifts of phosphorescent grass wedged tight among the grand gears overhead. The glimmer was sufficient to reveal the house was broken around her; a ring of masonry and splintered wood that sighed and settled like a dog lying down to sleep. Only the lift car in which she knelt was still in one piece.

She pressed one hand to the vial resting over her heart, anxious that it might have broken, but it was undamaged. She laughed, then, brushing dust from her hair, and stepped out of the brass cage. Aithan would be waiting.

Clambering over the mound of debris was more difficult than she anticipated. She reached the other side and sat for a moment on the thick moss to catch her breath. It was warmer than aboveground, but the air was not gritty with the taste of coal. Overhead the gears whirred and ticked; pumps pushed water into vast oceans and rushing rivers; massive ductwork funneled heat into the southern countries and drew it away from the icy plains; the whole mass of gears slowly turning Aboveworld around the central point of Underworld. All of it a familiar rhythm she hadn't realized she longed for.

There were lights in the distance; barely a spark in the shifting dark-that-wasn't-dark, but she knew it was Aithan's house. Just the thought made her heart beat faster. It used to be their house. *My house.*

She dug her fingers into the moss and whistled through her teeth. A metallic beetle emerged from the curling mass, then another and another, piling into a mound as large as she was. She pointed toward the distant building. "Take me home."

They skittered forward with the sound of coins being poured from a jar and latched onto her dress, shoes and hair till she was cloaked in copper. Tiny wings snapped open and beat the air, lifting her from the ground just as the others had done with Bás. Slowly, moving in currents she couldn't discern, they flew toward the house, depositing her at last on the doorstep.

Her hand trembled as she laid it on the doorknob. *Maybe it's locked.* It turned easily under her fingers, the door swinging open, silent.

She stomped into the hall, ready to face Aithan, but it was empty. The *tap-tap-tap* of her footsteps drifted into the darkness and did not return. "Hello?" The word also rattled away into nothing. Sephie scowled. "I've come home."

After a moment, a whisper came back to her, deeper than her own cracked voice. "Home."

She waited, but the hall remained empty. Forlorn. The mirrors were flaking, dust hung in cobwebbed tendrils from the dark chandelier. Sephie rubbed her hands together. It was colder than she remembered and for a moment she was afraid.

A thread of melody drifted from upstairs. Something melancholy.

Taking a deep breath, she went up the steps.

Aithan's study was in worse condition than the downstairs hall. The books were toppled from shelves, moldering beneath a coverlet of dust; the furniture was broken at every joint and the acrid smell of mold hung in the air.

Sephie squinted against the murk. "Aithan?"

Near the fireplace something moved, then a lamp flickered on. Aithan was less kempt than she remembered, but the decay that infected the house didn't seem to have touched him.

"Sephie." He stared at her, wide-eyed. "I thought I heard your voice, but I often think..." Shoving a pile of newspaper out of the way, he stepped close. "It *is* you."

"Yes."

"You've come home."

She nodded.

"You must hate me."

"I do."

"I know I did a terrible thing, but I was so angry. So hurt." He had gotten better at lying; there were even tears in his eyes. Or perhaps he was genuinely sorry.

Sephie didn't care. "What you did to me was horrible enough. But Bás…"

"I couldn't let him make a cuckold out of me like that. To allow a mortal to sully my wife and remain unpunished." The blood filled his cheeks as his hands moved across her body, possessive. "You I could forgive, but never him."

"We were not even lovers, Aithan." She waited, knowing he was clever enough to catch it.

"Were not?" Anger etched lines in the broad slab of his forehead. "And now?"

She laughed. "You thought I would bear the punishment without tasting the fruit?"

"You would never risk further punishment."

"No?" She pressed her lips against his, slipping her tongue into his mouth.

He groaned and his cock hardened, a taut peak under her fingers. "Persephone." He whispered her name mournfully, like a cold wind moaning over sea cliffs.

She touched her cheek to his, lips trembling by his ear. "Can you taste him?"

Aithan struck her hard enough that her knees gave out. "Whore."

Sephie wiped the blood from her lip. "You made me so. Husband. Because of you, I took him as a lover and gave back to him the thing you took."

He looked suddenly amused. "You brought him back to life?

You are a stupid little thing." He pulled her upright, fingers knotted in her hair. "The mortal mind cannot take such a strain. He will live, but wild and sick."

"You lie."

"No." He looked at her close. "But I think, deep down you care not at all for him."

She pressed her hand to her breast and the glass vial nestled there. "Perhaps." The pomegranate seeds trembled under her fingers. "Perhaps I have only ever thought of you and serving you as you served me."

The vial chimed as it broke, roots and slender threads of saplings uncurling from each of the seeds. Sephie gasped as the fabric of her dress tore open and the roots pierced her through, spilling blood that they drank freely.

The trees grew, branches punching through the ceiling, roots splitting open the floor. Sephie melted into the new flesh of the pomegranate grove. Her body shattered and was absorbed, but her soul settled in the central tree. She grew tall and strong. The house crumbled beneath her mighty limbs and she rustled her leaves in delight.

Something at her feet wailed. *Aithan.* Her roots wound around him and drew him inside. His magic flared, a desperate attempt to wither her into dust, but there was too much life in her; the whole current of the world flowed up through her feet and new roots wrapped him tight and tighter till he was soft and quiet.

The trees sighed, content.

"What of that one? He is new." The doctor gestured to the patient in the farthest bed.

The nurse nodded. "Mad as a hatter. And been through hell."

"A soldier?"

"Hard to say. We found him in the streets, dirty and broken. He'll not give us a name, only talks of a woman."

The doctor leaned over the patient. "Can you tell me who you are?"

"Apples." The man writhed against the straps holding him to the bed. "She tasted of apples."

The nurse raised a knowing eyebrow. "Always the same."

"Who tasted like apples?" The doctor was young and not so easily deterred.

"Sephie." His eyes were terribly bright. "Her last kiss..." Hands twitching against the rough mattress as though he would write something.

"What about her last kiss?"

The patient laughed. "It was hard. The last one always is." He fell back on the cot, twisting like a bit of grass caught in a slow fire.

"That's all you'll get from him." The nurse pulled the blanket up over him. "He's mad as death."

Zapada Alba

Tracey Lander-Garrett

In Romania, it is said the winter has no heart, but lungs of ice to breathe upon the young, the weak and the old. Many years ago, it was also said that winter had claimed Zapada Alba as his bride and frozen the girl at the height of her beauty, such that, even after death, she appeared only to sleep, her skin as white as snow, her lips like fallen rubies, her hair dark like the sky at midnight. They said the wolves howling were in mourning, because she had freed one of them from a hunter's trap the winter before. He had watched over her in gratitude, but not well enough.

Six wizened men struggled through the winter dusk, bearing on their shoulders a long wooden box. One ranged ahead with a machete, rending dead vines and dried roots, clearing a path for his brothers. Snow had not fallen in weeks, and rain had melted through all but the thickest drifts, now left like white islands in the rotting leaves on the forest floor. Skeletal branches caught at their brown and black clothing as they passed, yet still they slogged on, their grim unshaven faces hollow cheeked, sunken eyed.

The full moon rose upon the pine-shrouded clearing. Seven men stood with heads bowed, surrounding the box. It had been set upon stones, broad gray granite, the type used for building foundations, churches. The men stood as monuments while the moon climbed the arc of the sky. The pines created a circular room of the glen. Directly overhead, the moon lit the glade like a chandelier, stars catching its light like flickering chips of glass in the sky's ceiling. The moon's pale reflection was caught in the pane of glass set in the coffin lid. The cry of a wolf pierced the silence. One by one the men approached the box; each touched that pale mirror with a paler hand, then left the clearing.

A chill wind blew from the north. The night grew cold, and colder. A cloying cemetery darkness surrounded the bier where they had left her. They had been gone perhaps an hour when the heavily cloaked man approached, leading a dark horse into the clearing by its bridle.

She was as beautiful as the tales described: her ivory skin, hair as black as a raven's wing, blood-red lips half parted as though in anticipation of a kiss. She could not have been any older than seventeen, perhaps eighteen when she was taken; innocence still trembled beneath her still features.

The milky-white skin of her bosom made him tremble with impatience. He could see no more, for the glass stopped at her breast. His horse snorted and pawed the half-frozen ground, billows of fog blossoming from its nostrils. "Soon," the man said, reaching to lift the latch on the coffin side. Long tapered fingers dexterously loosed the ring from its post, and the wooden lid raised silently on well-oiled hinges. "Soon," he breathed once more.

They had not bothered to clothe her before sealing her in the box, and his intake of breath was ragged. No one had suspected; she remained whole, unmarked. The mounds of her breasts were of the finest porcelain, her nipples crimson like her lips. He closed his eyes a moment, then gently slid one hand beneath her neck, the other beneath the smallness of her waist, then down to cup her buttocks, and lifted her from the box. He cradled her there in his arms a moment. Her skin was cold, but pliable and soft as he laid her down onto the ground. He throbbed with his desire for her, the thickening of his turgid member becoming an ache as he caressed first her breasts, then the silk of her mound, and finally the cleft between her sweet legs. He fell on her then, wresting his clothes aside, pulling her thighs apart, launching himself inside her, pushing himself wildly against her, until he was spent.

He slowly raised himself onto one elbow, then the other, and drew himself from her in one long motion as he stood. After adjusting his clothing, he drew a handkerchief from one pocket and tenderly dried the peach halves of her sex, left split and shining from his ministrations. "Now, my sweet," he murmured, and gently drew her up once more, wrapping her in his cloak and placing her before him on the horse.

Hours passed. Snow fell, at first like tufts of milkweed, hanging in the air, almost suspended by the wind, then clinging to him, the horse, the girl; then it began to fall in a deluge, so thick that he could barely see. He was thankful for the snow because it would cover all traces of their passage. The horse knew its way back and had once returned to the castle with its coat singed and eyes swollen shut after having been struck by lightning.

The muffled clatter of the horse's hooves into the silent courtyard would have alerted even the dimmest of servants, but no one greeted him as he brought home his prize. He swung down from the horse and lifted her from the saddle, carrying the limp girl over the threshold and up the curving staircase.

He pushed open the door to a bedroom and set her down upon a red velvet coverlet, still enveloped in his cloak. Snowflakes hung in her hair like tiny seed pearls, seen in a pale slice of light coming through the curtains. "Exquisite," he murmured, and leaned down to claim a kiss from those lips. He hovered an inch above them, then placed his lips upon her forehead instead, as one might kiss a child. "Soon," he said once again, crossing the room to close the curtain. He then turned on his heel and left the room.

When he returned to her, the sun had crossed the sky and sunk once again beneath the edge of the world. He carried a candelabra and a white silk nightgown chased with lace at the bodice and hem. Placing the candelabra on a bedside table, he pulled his cloak from her and once again marveled at the perfection of her white skin, the voluptuousness of her breasts in comparison with her tiny waist and slim hips. Her feet and hands were petite, the nails pearlescent and dainty. This time he controlled his lascivious urges and raised her to a sitting position. Delicately, he pulled the nightgown over her head, eased each arm through its sleeve, and rolled the material over her breasts, letting it fall to her waist, then laid her back upon the bed, and raising her buttocks, pulled the gown over her legs as well.

He sat down beside her, plumping the pillows behind her head. The room was dark except for the flickering candles. Then, dragging a sharpened fingernail across the pad of his index finger, he leaned over her. A bead of blood appeared there and he applied pressure beneath the wound to force the blood's flow. "Now my darling," he whispered hoarsely, "now drink."

First the red lips parted and the little red tongue slipped

between them to lap at his finger as the bead trickled into her mouth. Then the lips closed around the tip of his finger, drawing it slowly into her mouth as she suckled, using her tongue and teeth to pull it in farther. A soft moan came from him, and he pricked another finger, pulling a line of blood across her bottom lip. She opened her mouth to accommodate the new finger, pulling it in next to its brother for several minutes. When he tried to pull them out she made a small mewling sound of discontent, but finally released him. Her mouth remained open this time, her lips moist and ripe as the red flesh of a pomegranate. He slashed his wrist in the same method as before and pressed it to those eager lips. Her eyes flew open, eyes the color of dark sapphires, the blue of the sky just before it turns to black. As she drew on the wound, color suffused her cheeks, and her breast began to rise and fall with passionate frequency. He moaned again, this time louder, and his wrist shifted in her grasp. A feral growl vibrated from her lungs as she bit harder, deeper, clutching the wrist with both hands so that he could not pull it away. The muscles in his arm flexed and pulsed beneath her hands, and her eyes, which had previously, though open, not *seen*, suddenly saw the reflection of her bridegroom in the mirror on the ceiling. Her eyes grew wide.

The man above her was bestial, furred, with sharp fingernails like claws and strange, golden, glowing eyes. Even now his transformation was incomplete; even now the dark gray fur had only begun to creep across his features, his nose beginning to lengthen into a snout, his body collapsing into the long sinews, the forelegs, the paws of the *loup garou*, the wolf, as his bride looked on, the copper taste of his blood in her mouth.

She released his wrist—no, no longer wrist, but foreleg—from her mouth and screamed once, loudly, rolling to the floor, bent in half, knees touching her forehead as she convulsed on the carpet. She shrieked again, longer and louder this time, as though the sound was being ripped from her lungs. The wolf leaped from the bed to her side while she screamed, and she made no move to escape it.

The animal whined softly and pushed his nose into her hair, licking gently at her face, licking the tears that had run down her cheeks. She whimpered, trying to hold back another scream that erupted from her throat. She could feel the soft roughness of his fur against her cheek, feel his hot breath in her hair, and still the taste of blood permeated her mouth.

She grabbed the sleek gray-furred body with a strength and speed that surprised her, and was surprised too, when she found herself sinking her teeth into the soft flesh of his throat. When she opened her eyes to look into the mirror above them again, her lover lay against her, spent, still furred, and her own eyes had turned ice blue.

She watched in the mirror as she grew black fur, watched her body grow tighter, her face grow longer, her sharp teeth grow sharper as she learned what it was to have four legs. She threw back her head and howled, and her lover howled with her. He took her then, from behind, and he watched as they each found their own skin again when he was through.

"My wolf," she murmured. "Trapped by love, but by no man."

"And my Zapada Alba, as beautiful dead as when you were alive, with skin as white as snow and fur as black as coal."

When the moon is full, Count and Countess Wolf run through the pines, branches catching at their coats, while snow falls softly from the sky.

AFTERWORD

Rachel Caine

I grew up on dark, Gothic tales of romance and danger and death...tremendous stories fraught with terror. I loved them, and yet I also often found that there was something missing. There was always the undercurrent that went hand in hand with fear and darkness: *sex*. An exciting and unspoken dark mystery kept in the shadows and behind carefully closed doors, as if it had to be contained for our safety. Sex drove plots and plans and revenge, but like the ghosts that haunted the halls, or the monsters creeping in the shadows, it was never to be seen straight on—only in sidewise glimpses, whispers and the tingles the ideas woke deep inside.

We know that real Victorian society was *intensely* sexual, yet had very definite roles. Women were saints or sinners; the saints were wives who were expected to do their duty, while the sinners were mistresses and ladies of the night, ready to take their wanton pleasures without shame. Men lived in both worlds, moving between the two, and while it was technically wrong, it was utterly mundane for a man of property to keep a mistress on the side. At night even the most upright family man might frequent brothels, collect pornographic cards or chase the opium dragon. Through such intense divisions came conflict— the daytime world colliding with the night, in the same way that horror crept out of shadows and alleys and crypts. There were consequences to hiding these things. Sometimes, they were fatal.

And yet, it's biology. We all secretly crave sex and pleasure in all its forms. It's part of the human condition, and we ignore that drive, that *need,* at our peril. In these modern times we can safely acknowledge a woman's sexuality and its power, and honestly examine how it changes and shapes the world around us.

We can also take a new look back at our Gothic past, with all its secrets and shadows, and unlock those closed doors, peek into the shadows and find even richer material to explore.

In this collection's great dark tales of sex and murder, fear and love, pain and pleasure, we see not only ourselves, but we also shine a candle on our collective past, and that is a powerful and exciting journey.

I invite you to go with us into darkness. It hides horrors and delights beyond your imagination.

And if the candle goes out...surrender to the dark.

Rachel Caine
Author of the Morganville Vampires series

About
the Authors

BENJI BRIGHT is the pen name of Bendi Barrett, a poet whose work has been in *PANK, Sein Und Werden,* and recently *Glitterwolf.* As Benji Bright he has published erotica with JMS Books, Queer Young Cowboys and Circlet Press. He is a graduate of Cornell University and lives near Chicago.

RACHEL CAINE is the author of more than forty novels, including the internationally bestselling Morganville Vampires series in young adult. She makes her home in Fort Worth, Texas with her husband, fantasy artist R. Cat Conrad, where she specializes in making the neighbors think all writers are weird.

ROSE DE FER is an English writer who loves the Gothic and decadent. Her novella *Lust Ever After* (Mischief Books) is a sexy re-imagining of *Bride of Frankenstein.* Other stories appear in *Red Velvet and Absinthe* (edited by Mitzi Szereto), and in numerous Mischief anthologies including *Underworlds, Submission* and *Forever Bound.*

KATE DOUGLAS's first erotic romance was published in 2001 and she has since had almost fifty erotic novels and novellas published by both small press and traditional publishers, along with a dozen other stories for a more conventional audience. She and her husband of over four decades live in Healdsburg, California.

CAIRDE GLASS is an author living in the southeastern United States. Her speculative fiction has been published at *Daily Science Fiction*, *Abyss & Apex*, and *The Beast Within 4: Gears and Growls*. She's currently querying a steampunk novel about magic, machinery and murder.

SACCHI GREEN writes erotica in western Massachusetts. Her alter ego Connie Wilkins writes speculative fiction, but the lines frequently get blurred. Sacchi's stories appear in scores of anthologies, including Mitzi Szereto's *Wicked: Sexy Tales of Legendary Lovers* and *Thrones of Desire*, and she's edited nine erotica anthologies herself, winning both Lambda and GCLS Awards.

KIM KNOX (kim-knox.co.uk) is an author of science fiction, fantasy and paranormal erotic and sensual romance. She's published by Carina Press, Ellora's Cave, Samhain Publishing, Entangled Publishing, Cleis and others. Her story "At the Sorcerer's Command" appeared in Mitzi Szereto's *Thrones of Desire*. She lives in northwest England.

TRACEY LANDER-GARRETT teaches in the English Department at Borough of Manhattan Community College and plays *Dungeons & Dragons* in her spare time. Most recently, she's published poetry and creative nonfiction in *Connotation Press* and *Electric Windmill Press*. She lives in Brooklyn, New York with her husband and too many cats.

ADRIAN LUDENS lives in the Black Hills of South Dakota. His mystery and horror tales have appeared in *Alfred Hitchcock's Mystery Magazine*, *Big Pulp*, *Blood Lite 3: Aftertaste*, *Diabolic Tales 3* and *Blood Rites*. His collection, *Bedtime Stories for Carrion Beetles*, is available on Amazon in multiple formats.

T. C. MILL (tc-mill.com) grew up in Wisconsin. Her short stories have been published by Circlet Press and Every Night Erotica, and she has e-books available from Dreamspinner, Storm Moon Press and Carina.

GARY EARL ROSS, retired University of Buffalo professor, is a novelist and playwright whose works include *Wheel of Desire*, *Shimmerville*, *Blackbird Rising*, *Picture Perfect*, *Murder Squared*, *The Scavenger's Daughter* and *Matter of Intent* (winner of the Best Play Edgar Award from Mystery Writers of America).

MADELEINE SWANN's erotica has appeared at the *Forbidden Fiction* website and in *The Big Book of Bizarro* anthology, and her surreal comedy and horror in *Polluto* magazine, Black Petal magazine, and from LegumeMan Books. She writes from her home in Essex, England.

ZANDER VYNE's (zandervyne.com) work is published in several genres. Her literary erotica is featured in Mitzi Szereto's

Red Velvet and Absinthe and *Thrones of Desire*. Chief editor at Full Sail Editing, she lives in Chicago, Illinois with her husband, daughter and an adopted Basenji mutt named Riley.

JO WU attends UC Berkeley, where she studies biology and creative writing, and writes for the award-winning *Caliber Magazine*. Her work has appeared in *Gothology II: Misery Loves Company*, *Underneath the Juniper Tree* and Mitzi Szereto's *Thrones of Desire*. She also models in magazines under the alias Carmilla Jo.

ROSALÍA ZIZZO is a hot-blooded Sicilian whose work has appeared on several online sites and in a number of anthologies, including *Best Women's Erotica 2012* and *2013*, *Stretched* and *Santa's Hot Secrets*. A former teacher, she holds a BA in comparative literature from UC Davis and now lives in Rocklin, California.

ABOUT
THE EDITOR

MITZI SZERETO (mitziszereto.com) is an author and anthology editor of multi-genre fiction and nonfiction. She has her own blog, Errant Ramblings: Mitzi Szereto's Weblog (mitziszereto.com/blog) and a Web TV channel, Mitzi TV (mitziszereto.com/tv), which covers the "quirky" side of London. Her books include *The Wilde Passions of Dorian Gray* (a sequel to Oscar Wilde's classic novel); the epic fantasy anthology *Thrones of Desire: Erotic Tales of Swords, Mist and Fire*; the crime/cozy mystery *Normal for Norfolk (The Thelonious T. Bear Chronicles)*; the Jane Austen sex parody *Pride and Prejudice: Hidden Lusts*; *Red Velvet and Absinthe: Paranormal Erotic Romance*; *In Sleeping Beauty's Bed: Erotic Fairy Tales*; *Getting Even: Revenge Stories*; *Wicked: Sexy Tales of Legendary Lovers*; *Dying For It: Tales of Sex and Death*; the *Erotic Travel Tales* anthologies and many other titles. A popular social media personality and frequent interviewee, she's known for having pioneered erotic writing workshops in the United Kingdom and mainland Europe and has lectured in creative writing at several British universities. Her anthology *Erotic Travel Tales 2* is the first anthology of erotica to feature a Fellow of the Royal Society of Literature. Her next book will be *Love, Lust and Zombies*. She divides her time between London, England and various locations in the United States.